MW01243776

THE DRAGON KING

AN ELEMENTAL SPIN-OFF

THE ELEMENTAL
BOOK 2

T. B. WIESE

Copyright © 2022 by T. B. Wiese

1-1149740421I TX 9-149-320

All rights reserved.

No part of this book may be reproduced in any form or by any electronic or mechanical means, including information storage and retrieval systems, without written permission from the author, except for the use of brief quotations in a book review.

Cover Design by T. B. Wiese

ISBN: 979-8-9858850-4-0

Image license: 1144577175

❀ Created with Vellum

For everyone whose favorite character from The Elemental was Kem.

OTHER BOOKS IN THIS WORLD

AUTHOR'S NOTE

The Dragon King is a dark paranormal romance with dragon shifters. This novella contains elements of graphic violence (murder, blood, fighting, gore, dismemberment ...), dealing with loss of family, swearing, sex (graphic scenes, magic used as toys, dark themes), non-consent, being drugged, attempted sexual assault, and kidnapping.

1

KEMREMIR

I ANGLE my wings to catch the draft, and I'm lifted higher into the endless blue sky. My shadows trail my body, the smoky tendrils twisting around my tail as I shift it slightly to adjust my direction. Breathing deep, the scents of mountain air and lilac relax my muscles. Right now, I have no agenda, no duties to fulfill. I'm simply enjoying the peace that always comes from flying over my kingdom.

I tilt my massive wings and dive toward the edge of the mountain. There's the place I first brought Raelyn, the Seelie princess. I huff a chuckle, a small stream of smoke billowing from my lips. She's now the Seelie Queen, and that assassin scoundrel, Asheraht, is now her king.

My talons curl loosely, the tips brushing the blue-green grass of the mountain meadow. The vibrant yellow sandril flowers are absent this time of year. The snows are coming, and the Moneria celebration will usher in the new year in honor of the goddess of the mountains.

I bank hard; the wind pulling on my wings, the muscles of my back straining against the drag. The rush of the waterfall flashes past, the spray sparkling against my black scales, the cloud of mist curling around me. An easy roll turns me over, and I'm once again spiraling into the sky, the winter sun turning the water on my scales to shimmering diamonds.

My scales ripple as I shake from head to tail, flinging the droplets out around me. I slow, tilting my body upright, my wings spread wide. Then I'm hanging in suspension, weightless, looking down on all that is mine—mine by right of Challenge.

I hang, breathless, grateful, exhilarated, and overwhelmed by the sheer beauty of my land ... and then I'm falling. I tuck my wings tight, rotating until I'm pointed like an arrow toward the ground. The pull of the wind against my face causes my second lid to slide over my eyes. The blue-green of the mountain grass turns to a bright red as the valley draws closer. Gravity presses in on my bones, the molten fire in my veins compressing and boiling as my heart struggles to beat against the crush of my dive.

Joy. This is joy.

A laugh erupts from my chest, coming out as a roar that shakes the ground as I snap out my wings and pull up at the last second. The adrenaline rush of the dive mellows into a gentle peace as I once again float along the valley floor toward my castle.

Crystal, marble and glass reflect the many colors of my kingdom, and smug pride curls my lips up in what I know is a fearsome smile. I earned this. By might, by strength, by winning Challenge after Challenge. I have the scars to prove my worth.

I am King of the Dragons of The Realm of the Crimson Plains.

Circling my castle once, I gently flap my wings, slowing my speed, and a moment before my claws touch the gravel path of the royal gardens, I call up my magic and shift. It's as easy as breathing, allowing the warm rush of power to fold itself around me, like sinking into a mineral bath. My shadows condense, and with my next breath, my boots touch down, and my gentle momentum carries me forward into a slow walk.

I roll my shoulders, shaking off the last of my dragon, my inky shadows hugging my black skin, not yet ready to retreat. The scent of winter roses and lilac carries through the air as I lift my hand, watching the shadows curl and dance around my fingers. For the millionth time, I wish I knew more about my shadows, about my past, about my family. A dark mental cloud threatens to sweep away my good mood from my flight. No matter how hard I try to remember, no matter how many texts I research, there's nothing to be found about the black dragons, and certainly no mention of dragons with shadows. I have no recollection of my parents—the dragons of the valley clan found me by the North Lake and raised me. It's like someone dropped me out of the sky.

I'm lost in my thoughts, not paying attention to the path before me, and as I automatically take a turn around an evergreen hedge, I skid to a stop to avoid crashing into one of my guards.

Arvun's liquid silver eyes go wide as she shuffles back, bowing her head. Her short silver hair falls around her face. "I'm so sorry, your Majesty. I was searching for you and was told you were out flying."

"My fault. I wasn't paying attention. What can I do for you, Arvun?"

"You have a guest. She's waiting in the east solarium ... unless you'd rather have her escorted to the throne room?"

A little kick of joy flutters through my heart as I start walking down the path again, Arvun keeping stride one pace behind me.

"Raelyn?"

"No, my Lord. Syphe returned from Attolyn this morning. Queen Raelyn won't be able to make it today. She will try to reschedule for next week."

How does the earth saying go? I'm not surprised, just disappointed. But I know all too well how the responsibilities of ruling eat away at your time. I'll find the time to go see Rae if she can't make it here.

"Then, who? I'm not expecting any visitors from on or off world—speaking of which, is the next application voting session still on for this evening?"

"Yes, your Majesty. Unless ..." I draw to a stop, turning to face Arvun. Raising an eyebrow at her silence, I urge her to continue. "Unless ... you may need to postpone due to your guest."

Well, this is intriguing.

Sliding my hands into my pockets, I rock back on my heels. "So, who is it I'm about to meet?"

"Tatha, my Lord."

My brows pinch tighter as I try to place the name. Arvun catches my confusion and continues, "The Lady of the Mountain clan."

I hide my surprise and smooth out my face, resuming my slow pace back to the castle.

"When did she arrive?"

"Three hours ago, your Majesty. Would you prefer to meet her in the throne room?"

It's been years since a dragon from the Mountain clan

came down to the valley. I wonder what has drawn the Lady of the reclusive clan out of the safety of their home? Then another thought hits me.

"She's in her human form?"

Arvun nods. This mystery is just getting deeper. The mountain clan prefer not to shift from their true dragon form. My predecessor outlawed our dragon forms for many years to keep us under his control. When I took his throne by right of Challenge and lifted the ban, many dragons shifted and retreated to the mountains where they could live in their natural state at all times. We leave them in peace, and they keep to themselves.

Until now.

After nearly two-hundred-fifty years of seclusion, what has driven the Mountain clan to send Tatha down to the valley? I've never met the Mountain clan Lord's daughter. Curiosity and anticipation tingle across my scale-hard skin.

"I'll see her in the solarium. Thank you, Arvun."

She bows, stopping at the bottom step as I climb toward the glass doors to the great hall of my castle. Arvun calls up after me, "Shall I have refreshments sent, my Lord?"

I'm not sure if Tatha has ever worn her human form, and I'm sure being here is ... unsettling. Presenting her with unfamiliar human food might be too much for her.

"No. That is all."

The soft crunch of gravel under Arvun's shoes fades as she walks away to attend to her many other duties. Good help is hard to find, but I've been lucky.

My long strides take me down hall after hall, passing the occasional staff member or guard. A flash of red hair here, burnt orange there, sky blue, sapphire ... the colors of the dragons bleeding into their human forms to create a rainbow of people.

At the next turn, the double doors to the solarium come into view. They are wide open to the glass room beyond, the tropical plants within bursting with color year round. A small woman stands in the center of the room, her back to me.

My pace slows as I watch her delicate fingers caress the petals of a plumeria I brought back from earth. The brilliant pink blooms stand vibrant against her pale skin and purple nails. Amethyst purple hair cascades down just past her shoulders in soft waves and curls. It looks soft, like spun sugar.

But as I draw closer, I catch the shimmer of brilliant gold tips to her purple nails, and there's an occasional gold streak of hair running through her purple locks.

A duo-chrome dragon. So rare. The mystery of Tatha deepens.

The heavy, musty, floral scent of the solarium wafts out of the room, and I take a deep breath.

My feet stop, as if cemented to the floor. Every muscle goes rigid. My dragon fire roars through my veins, and my shadows peel from my skin, reaching out—-to her.

Her scent lingers here where she must have passed by hours ago, and it climbs down my nose. The urge to shift rips at me from the inside, like my dragon will claw me apart if I don't let it free. It wants me to force her shift. It wants me to sink my talons into her dragon's hide. My dragon NEEDS me to sink my teeth into her flesh in a claiming bite.

As her scent—fire, and cinnamon, and earth—covers my tongue and coats my throat, my beast roars within me.

MATE!

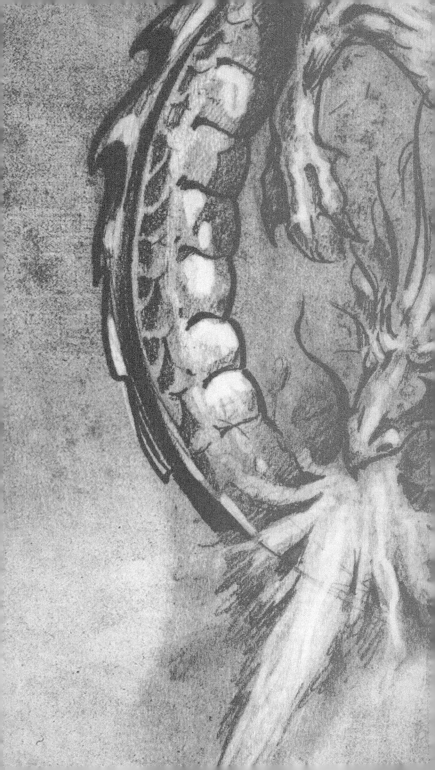

2

TATHA

I DON'T WANT to be here. My skin itches. I feel compressed. As a dragon, I'm fairly small, and that has bled into my petite human form. This is only the second time I've ever held my human form in all my one-hundred-eighteen years of life. Everything feels both too small and too large. I know I'm blinking too much, but the absence of my second lid feels wrong. Sounds seem muted, and I can't taste the air with this flat, human tongue.

I hate it.

The pink petals of the flower before me brush over my skin like silk. My eyes catch on the gold tips of my nails. I love my colors, but being the only duo-chrome dragon in the Mountain clan has brought me ... undue attention. That, along with my position as Lady of the clan, keeps me under the eye of my people, when I'd much rather disappear into my cozy nest with a good story.

I drop my hand, sighing. I've been wandering this sunlit room for over three hours. At first, the beautiful solarium transfixed me, and I was sure if I could get my hands on a stack of books, I could curl up on the plush sofa and be content here for days. But I don't have any books, and the novelty of the room has worn off.

Turning, intending to find someone to bring me a drink, or a book, or allow me to go to another room, I freeze. There stands the Dragon King. I blink several times. My eyes feel dry even in this humid room. He's tall, dark, and handsome if ever the description were made for someone. A tie holds back half of his black locs, showing off the sharp plains of his face. His black eyes watch me, the fiery-red centers burning with an intensity I don't understand. The silver of age dusts his beard, and though his hands are in his pockets and his posture is relaxed, there's a tension rolling off him. I swallow around the sudden dryness in my throat.

Realizing I've been staring, I quickly bend at the waist, bowing my head. "Your Majesty. I'm sorry for arriving with no notice or invitation. The matter is urgent, and I—"

"It's fine, Lady of the Mountain clan. I am honored by your presence."

His voice caresses me like a lover's whispered words. I clench my hands to keep a shiver from stealing down my spine. "It's Tatha, and it is I that am honored, Sire."

I stand, but when I take a step toward him, he backs up, keeping the distance between us, so I stop. Maybe it's bad form to approach the King without permission. Surely father would have told me if such a thing was taboo, but then again father is …

Chewing my lip, I glance around again. Being in this place makes my human skin crawl with unfamiliarity, but will the beautiful caves of my home still bring me comfort … after?

I clear my throat, blinking away the burn of tears I know won't fall. Standing a little taller, I watch King Kemremir, waiting. He's much bigger than I imagined, and the occasional curl of shadows around his dark skin adds to his larger-than-life energy. For a long moment, he just continues to stare. My fingers tap against the soft drape of my dress where it falls over my thighs. I have the urge to fidget, but I manage to hold still under the King's seemingly endless gaze.

Finally, he lifts an arm, gesturing deeper into the room. "Please, take a seat and tell me how I can help."

I turn, slowly making my way to the seating area, passing the overstuffed sofa to sit on the edge of one of the chairs. Its cushion is softer and deeper than I thought, and my body pitches back embarrassingly. I catch myself, adjusting to sit tall, but when I glance at the King, he's still standing where I left him.

Another moment passes where he just stares at me, then, skirting all the way around the sofa and other chairs, he lowers himself into the farthest seat from me with a grace that's surprising for a man so large. He barely seems to fit, his muscled thighs pressed to the inner arms of the chair.

He leans back, tapping a black nail on the chair, his eyes never leaving my face. "So, what can I do for you, Tatha?"

The sound of my name on his lips sends a curl of ... something through my belly. My skin feels too tight, and my claws want to burst from my small fingers. I blink fast and crack my jaw, trying to pop my ears, though I know that's not the issue —it's this form.

Shaking my head, I remember the King asked me a question. Sorrow hollows out my chest, and my words stick in my throat. I have to swallow several times before I manage to say, "My father is dying."

Genuine pain pinches the corners of Kemremir's eyes and

pulls his lips down in a small frown. His response chases away my own sorrow, and surprise takes its place. The King cares. My heart does a strange little flutter, but I ignore it as Kemremir's deep voice caresses the space between us.

"I knew he was ailing, but did not realize he was so far gone. Is there anything I can do to help ... to lengthen his time? I can send the royal healers to—-"

I shake my head. "No, your Majesty. Everything that can be done has been done. My father has kept the severity of his failing health a secret." I swallow around the ball of anger and sorrow. "Even from me, until recently." Sighing, I shake my head, refusing to relive the many arguments I've had with my father. "He's tired. He ... he's ready."

The King nods, his frown deepening. "I understand. Tovra is a great leader, and though I haven't seen him in many years, I will miss my friend."

Friend? My father and the King are friends?

He leans forward, bracing his muscular forearms on his thighs. "How long does he have?"

"Our healers say a week, maybe days."

Kemremir sits back and taps his nails on the chair again. "Have arrangements been made to bring him down to the North Lake for his Elevation?"

I shift in my chair.

"Actually, your Majesty, that is the main reason I came here today. My father wishes to be Elevated at the crest of our Mountain, and ..." I interlace my fingers, my gaze unfocused on my lap. "He requests you come to our Mountain to perform his Elevation when the time comes."

Silence greets me, and after a long pause, I look up to find the King's heavy gaze on me. At least the sadness has left his face, but in its place is ... what? His eyes look slightly wider, his fist is closed tight around the arm of his chair, and his head tilts to the side like he's trying to think of a way to get rid of me, or to eat me, and not in a good way.

A shiver spears down my spine at that unbidden thought, and a deep throbbing pulses low in my belly as if he physically ran his nails down my back. Wetness gathers between my thighs, and my skin goes hot. I hate being human—it's overwhelming.

Before either of us says another word, a new voice breaks the heavy silence, this one high and amused. "I heard the Lady of the Mountain had blessed us with her presence, and I just had to come see."

Kemremir's back goes stiff, and his eyes narrow. My head swivels around to see the newcomer. The man standing at the entrance of the solarium is tall, but nowhere near as tall as Kemremir. His spring-green hair is slicked back, reminding me of a mother that has licked back her youngling's hair.

His eyes rove my body as he continues, "But what do I overhear? The Mountain clan once again trying to throw off our laws. When was the last time your father actually attended a council meeting?"

His expensive clothes fit perfectly, highlighting his lean, sculpted body. There's a beauty to him, but it's like a hibibiscra flower—the bright red blooms will draw you in, but if you dare touch the petals, your skin will itch, burn, then bubble with blisters.

Something about this man screams to stay away, but his words rile me. Who does this pretentious dragon think he is? I sit taller. "It's actually not dragon law to be Elevated at North Lake, simply tradition."

The green-haired man smirks, his brow raising. "All the same, our traditions are sacred. The Mountain clan has grown too comfortable in their solitude."

A witty retort is on the tip of my tongue, but a low growl

rumbles from Kemremir, and I turn to find him standing. When did he move? He has maintained his distance but has positioned himself partially between the green-haired man and me. Wispy shadows curl away from the King's body like a black sun flare, and my lips part in awe. I've heard of his shadows, of course, but to see them in person is …

Kemremir's low voice peels my gaze back to his face. "Inchel, leave. You have insulted our guest with your presence and your words."

Inchel's lips pull up in a cruel smile as he leans a shoulder against the doorframe. His eyes land on me again, and I fight to keep from sinking into my chair as his gaze travels back down my body. He tilts his head, like he's assessing me. I sit taller, keeping my eyes on him. He snaps his gaze between the King and me a few times before his sharp tongue darts out and licks his lips with a small nod, coming to some conclusion.

Kemremir growls again, louder this time, and takes another step toward him.

Inchel raises a hand. "Of course, our mighty King will make an exception for the Mountain clan. I would too, for such a beauty."

Kemremir's shadows spread like dragon wings. The darkness expands, blocking my view of Inchel. I stand, clenching my fists at my side. I don't need protection.

But then I feel more than see the King turn slightly to face me. The inky shadows part, revealing his face. His eyes are creased at the edges with what I can only assume is concern, but there's also a small grin on his lips as he glances at my clenched fists. With a shake of his head, he turns back to Inchel, and his shadows draw back to his body, melting into his skin.

Amazing.

When Inchel comes back into view, I catch the wide-eyed look of fear on his face before he smooths his features into a smirk, mumbling, "This is most excellent." His eyes snap to me again, landing on my chest. I hold his gaze, anger at his disrespect straightening my spine and subsequently pressing my small chest against the thin fabric of my plain dress.

Shining scales crawl along Kemremir's black skin. His black nails elongate to sharp claws. Steam rises from his body, and I can practically feel his dragon fire pulsing through his veins. This dragon is more powerful than any I've encountered.

A long pause hangs in the air as heavy as the scents of the flowers and ferns around us.

Inchel's smile spreads to a malicious grin. "It is time, Kemremir."

I'm not sure why, but my skin bristles at Inchel's disrespect by calling our King by name. I take a step forward ... to do what? Jump to defend Kemremir's honor? If someone spoke to my father in such a tone, I'd be on them in a second, claws and teeth tearing and shredding. I may be small, but I've trained and fought all my life. I've taken down dragons over twice my size.

I plant my feet. The King doesn't need me. He doesn't need anyone. My teeth ache with the power pulsing off him. My eyes snap between the two men who obviously have a history, and not a great one, it seems.

Another growl rumbles from Kemremir, and my body heats at the sound. What is going on with me?

"Inchel, I don't have time for this right now. Leave."

"No, Kemremir." Inchel's eyes snap to mine. There's a wildness to him; excitement pulling his face into a slightly crazed look. "I Challenge you!"

For a second, I think he's Challenging me, but his heavy gaze crawls from my face, landing on Kemremir.

He's Challenging the King? My laugh bubbles from my lips before I can stop it. Inchel's head snaps back in my direction, his greedy smile sliding to a scowl. The King keeps his back to me, but I catch the faintest chuckle beneath his growl. I press my lips together. If Inchel's dragon is anything like the man, he could never best Kemremir.

And the King seems to share my amusement as his chuckle grows louder until he throws back his head and laughs. "Really, Inchel? Now? After all these years of threatening to Challenge me, you've finally found the balls to do it?"

Kemremir rolls his shoulders, glancing back at me, and for some reason, I have the urge to run to him and wrap my arms around his waist. But I bite the inside of my cheek, blink several times, and hold still. Being in my human form is messing with me. This was supposed to be a quick trip, but here I am, stuck between these two males.

Kemremir continues, "So, when would you like to die?"

He speaks the words like a promise, but Inchel's smile is back in place and doesn't waver as his eyes sweep over me yet again. "In deference to the Lady's father's failing health, I will allow you to see to his final days and to his Elevation."

There's not an ounce of sympathy in his voice, and I wonder what game he's playing.

Inchel turns back to Kemremir. "Enjoy your last days, black dragon. You will not be around to see the new year."

Kemremir says nothing.

Eyes on me, Inchel licks his lips again. "It was a pleasure to meet you ...." I don't give him my name, and neither does Kemremir, which I am grateful for. A little half-smile lights up Inchel's pretty face. "... Lady of the Mountain clan. I look forward to seeing you again at the Challenge."

Raising an eyebrow, I nod. "I look forward to it. I've always wanted to see the King fight. The stories are legendary."

Kemremir's eyes bore into mine, and there's something like hunger in their depths. I swallow, but Inchel's cruel chuckle draws my attention away from the King. "Legendary, yes. But legends fade." He bows to me, not Kemremir. "I look forward to working with your people as your new King."

That thought sours my stomach, and I dig my nails into my palms.

Inchel turns on his heels, his expensive shoes tapping loudly on the marble floor as he strides down the hall.

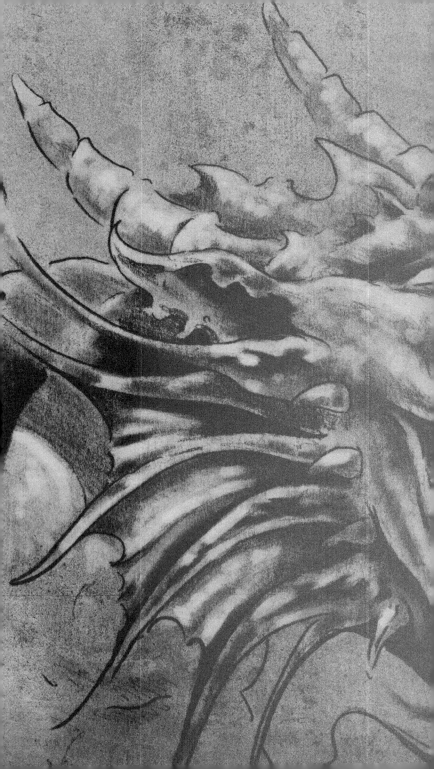

3

KEMREMIR

INCHEL WAS close to losing his head several times in the last few minutes—not over the Challenge, I'm not concerned in the least about that. It's the way he looked at Tatha. She's mine, or at least my dragon believes she's ours. And I'm inclined to agree.

Every moment in the solarium with her has been bliss and agony. There was a calm that settled in my soul by simply being near her, but the raging need to claim her had my cock half-hard, and I could barely focus on our conversation. Her voice was like a siren's song, and I had to concentrate to keep from getting lost in the melody.

At first, I wondered why she didn't react to me. We were certainly close enough for her to scent me, but then I noticed her eyes kept blinking too fast, and her hands fidgeted as she took alternating shallow and deep breaths.

Realization hit me then. Her human form is disturbing her

senses. She is overwhelmed—with her shift, with her father's failing health, with being in the castle, with meeting her king for the first time ... So I've kept as much distance as I can, trying to allow her to acclimate while fighting to keep my dragon from leaping on her and tearing that dress from her small body.

I keep an eye on Inchel until he turns a corner, and when I'm sure he's gone, I face Tatha. A gasp threatens to escape my throat as I once again take in her beauty. Her soft purple eyes, ringed with gold, watch me, occasionally glancing down the hall where Inchel walked off.

I clear my throat. "Sorry about that. I know you probably want to get back to your father, but is there any way I can convince you to stay for the evening? I'd like to speak with you about your clan and your father's wishes."

She bows before glancing up at me through the fall of her amethyst hair. The Mating call hits me like a physical punch to the chest, and I take a small step back, imagining her looking up at me like that right before she takes my cock into her mouth.

Her eyes crease as she straightens to her full height. Small but mighty. "That man just Challenged you! ... Sire. You don't need to worry about the Mountain clan right now."

I wave a hand, a lightness spreading through my chest at the heat and compassion in her voice. "Oh, don't worry about that. I will kill Inchel. His clan will select a new council representative, and life will go on."

Her eyes travel over my body, and every inch of my skin pebbles. When she makes it back to my face, a small smile lifts her lips. "So ... so, you will come to the Mountain, your Majesty?"

"Of course, Heilsi." The language of the ancients slides from my tongue, and I realize the name fits—Fierce one.

It's been centuries since the dragons have spoken the old language; new, more modern dialects taking its place. But every once in a while, our present-day words aren't enough —like now.

Her brows pinch, not understanding the word, but she bows again. "Thank you, your Majesty." Straightening, she drums her fingers against her thigh, the skirt of her dress shifting slightly with the movement. My shadows swirl around my hands, my fingers aching to inch that skirt up her legs until I'm able to scent her deep between her thighs.

At the sight of my shadows reaching for her, a little gasp passes between her lips, and the sound punches right to my cock. I back up another step, forcing my shadows to melt back into my skin. I smile at her, hoping I look calmer than I feel. "My shadows seem to like you."

Her eyes travel over my hands, up my arms, and across my chest. I have the urge to let the smokey tendrils back out for her.

She smiles. "They are ... beautiful." Tilting her head to the side, she asks, "What is their function?"

Beautiful? I've never seen them that way. They are a mystery. Sometimes, they are useful. They are what make me different.

I shrug with a soft chuckle. "I'm not sure. They're great for hiding in dark corners, and there's an intimidation factor that comes in handy sometimes, but on the whole, they're just ... there."

Her eyes drop back to the floor. "I shouldn't have asked. I'm sorry. Being different is something I understand."

My feet take two steps toward her without my permission before I'm able to stop. "Don't apologize, Heilsi. Not to me. Never to me. If there is something you want to know, ask."

Her head lifts. "What does that—"

She halts her question, her eyes dancing between mine. I take another step back, my shoulder brushing along the deep green leaves of the tardina plant, the fragrant shrub temporarily drowning out Tatha's spicy scent, allowing my dragon to relax, just slightly. When she doesn't finish her question, I ask, "Will you stay?"

"If you wish, your Majesty."

Oh, I wish for so much from her. But I'll start with dinner.

"Thank you, Tatha. I'll have a room readied for you. You are welcome to wander the castle if you desire. Any areas off limits are locked, so feel free to explore."

Her eyes light up, and I have the feeling a locked door will only present a challenge for her. I hold back my grin as she rolls her shoulders, looking up through the glass ceiling. "If it's okay with you, Sire, I'd like to fly."

"Of course. I'll have dinner prepared. It will be ready at your leisure."

"That's not necessary, your Majesty. I can catch something while I'm out."

I shake my head. "I'd like the opportunity to get to know you over a meal. Eating as a human is an … experience."

She bites her lip, and I can tell she doesn't like the idea of eating cooked food, or maybe the idea of eating with me makes her nervous—or both. But she nods, tucking her hair behind her ear. "Then I won't be long, your Majesty."

"Kem."

"What?"

"Call me Kem. And take your time. Flying through the valley is one of my favorite things to do."

How I'd love to scream through the air currents around the mountains with her. I'd love to drag my wings through the waterfall, sending a spray of mist onto her purple scales.

Her head whips back and forth. "Oh, I can't possibly call you ... it's improper, your Majesty."

I chuckle. "Humor me? At least when we are alone?"

She raises an eyebrow. "Okay ... Kem."

My eyes almost roll back in my head at the sound of my name on her lips. Fuck. I'm in trouble. I'd go for a flight of my own to cool off, but I can't chance running into her in the skies. My dragon would sink his claws into her, mount her, and ride her in a free-fall until she climaxes.

I take another step back, crossing the threshold. "Thank you, Tatha. Enjoy your flight. A staff member will bring you to dinner when you're ready."

Turning, I keep my pace casual, when all I want to do is run away ... or run back to her and crush my lips to hers. Rounding a corner, I press my back to a wall and run my hand over my face. Letting out a deep breath, I shove off the wall. Absently, my feet take me through my castle, aiming for the south wing to the large salt-water pool. I prefer the lake on the far side of the valley, but ... Tatha.

The sound of my boots against the marble is distant in my ears, the gleam of the crystal walls shimmers in my periphery. But my mind can't appreciate the beauty of my surroundings. All I can think of is *her*. My Mate. I found her—or rather; she came to me. All this time, she's been in the mountains.

I have a Mate. The one soul in the universe meant for me. And the call to claim her is strong.

Pulling my shirt over my head, I kick off my boots and step out of my pants. I dive into the pool, the cool water slicing over my heated skin, and thoughts of Tatha naked and swimming with me play out in my mind.

Finding an easy rhythm, I attempt to swim away from my raging desire. My shoulders flex as my arms cut through the water. My legs kick powerfully, and with every lap, my pace picks up.

Stroke, stroke, stroke, breath. Stroke, stroke, stroke, breath.

I dive deep, blowing the air from my lungs. Hitting the bottom, I turn over and lay on my back. The water ripples above me, the refracted light hypnotizing. But then movement catches my eye.

A smirk pulls across my face as I see a flash of bronze hair that moves out of sight, then back again, then out of sight ... over and over.

I push against the floor of the pool, shooting for the surface, and when my head breaks out of the water, I spy my guard, Syphe, pacing back and forth.

On her next pass, she notices I've surfaced, and a rumble vibrates from her chest as her lips pull back with rage. "That slimy worm! That useless bag of meat! How dare he! Ugh! That mother-fucker! Oily, green sludge of a dragon!"

Her tirade continues as I press my palms to the edge of the pool and haul myself out, shaking the water from my body. A towel hits me in the face as Syphe continues swearing creatively.

"Syphe, calm do—" She stops, spins, and slams her stare at me. I chuckle, holding up a hand in peace. "Inchel is a mild annoyance. His timing is shit, but—"

"Oh! What did the Lady of the Mountain clan want?" The fight temporarily leaves her as curiosity takes its place.

My frown reflects my change in mood, even as my stomach muscles clench as Tatha's image floats through my mind. I secure the towel around my waist, padding over to my pile of clothes. "Tovra is dying."

A small sound of sorrow comes from Syphe, and she paces again. "He will be missed. Will his daughter take his place as clan leader?"

"I'm not sure, but I'm meeting with her again over dinner. We will sort out as much as we can tonight. Then I'll leave with her in the morning for the mountains. I will see Tovra through his last days. He wishes to be Elevated on the Mountain." I pull on my clothes, my muscles loose after my time in the pool.

Syphe pauses, hands on hips. "Makes sense. But what of the Challenge?"

That last word comes out on a growl, and I smile, sliding on my boots. "It's Inchel. I'm not worried."

She raises an eyebrow. "You know he'll try something."

"Of course. He can't beat me if he doesn't cheat." I cross to Syphe, placing a hand on her muscled shoulder. "I'll still win."

Her breath leaves her in a great sigh, and a slow grin lights up her face. "I know. But why now?"

I shrug, clapping a hand to Syphe's back. "Who knows? He's been after the crown for years." My fists clench. "He did seem overly interested in Tatha."

"Maybe he's trying to make an impression?"

"If so, it's wasted on her."

She tilts her head at me as we move together out of the pool room. I pull my locs back, squeezing the water from my hair. "I trust you'll keep everything in order while I'm in the mountains."

"Of course, Sire."

"Do you and Bran have any plans for Moneria?"

A blush colors Syphe's skin at the mention of her Mate, and her fingers play with the leather and bronze Mating cuff on her left wrist. Syphe is one of the lucky few to have found her fated Mate. And now I'm among those small numbers.

"No. Not really. We plan to attend the planting of the seed, maybe a drink or two, but we really just want to ring in the new year at home."

"In each other's arms."

Her lips press into a cute smile, but then a scowl drops in place, her bronze eyes flaring with rage once again. "If that green mucus sack ruins Moneria, I'll ..." She glances at me, a flash of fear widening her eyes slightly.

"I won't tell you not to worry, because I know you will. But trust me, Syphe. I've fought and won thirty-seven Challenges. Soon to be thirty-eight."

She shakes her head, a small smile coming back to her face. "Well, just so you know, if the unthinkable happens, I'll Challenge Inchel immediately and take back your kingdom."

"I'm both flattered and insulted."

Our shared laughter floats down the hall, bouncing off the burnt-gold crystal walls that reflect the last rays of the sun.

"Go have dinner with your Mate, Syphe. I'll see you when I return, and we will toast my win over a drink at the Moneria celebration."

And if I have my way, I'll be whisking my own Mate to my bed to bring in the new year properly.

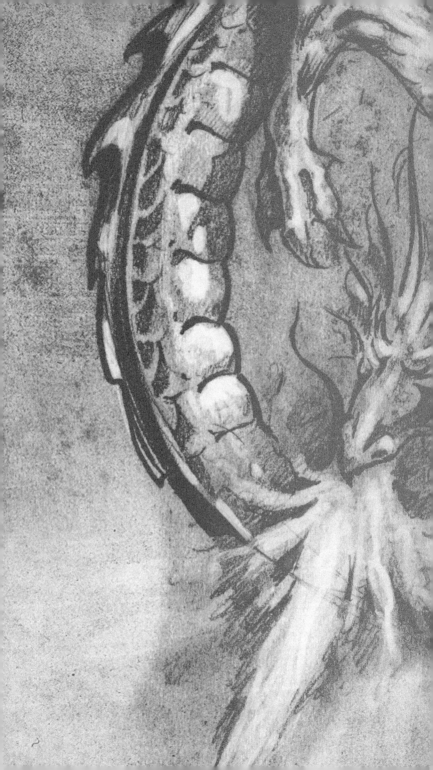

4

TATHA

THE HOURS of tense muscles and muted senses disappear as soon as my Dragon tingles over my skin and my wings spread wide. My forked tongue licks the air, tasting snow from the mountains. Home calls to me, and the image of my father curled in his nest deep in our beautifully carved caves tightens my chest.

Launching off the ground, I'm airborne. The beauty of the valley steals my attention, distracting me from the painful thoughts of my father. The red grass waves and bends under the currents created by my wings. My talons dip in the large east lake, leaving ripples in my wake. I dance around the large, fluffy clouds, the mist clinging to my body, glimmering over my gold-flecked purple scales. And when I burst from the clouds, throwing my wings wide, the soft light of the setting sun reflects off my body as I hang in suspension for a long moment.

I fly for a full hour before touching back down outside the border of the castle gardens. The sharp pull of my dragon melting into my human form scratches at my skin, and my eyes immediately start burning again without my second lid. But the peace and relaxation from my flight stays with me, like a sun-warmed blanket.

My soft boots make little sound as I cross the gravel paths of the gardens, brushing my hand over the evergreens and winter roses. We don't have these varieties high in the mountains, and their beauty in the face of winter is captivating.

Stepping back into the castle, I brace for that closed-in feeling, but it's not as bad as earlier today. The caves within my Mountain are vast, and though the castle is grand, it seems tiny compared to my home. But the crystal walls and exorbitant windows make the structure feel open and airy.

Pausing in a hallway, I press my fingers to the wall, the cool smoky crystal almost glowing with the last rays of the sun. I ... like it—this place. It feels ... I can't place it, but it's like a cool dip in water on a hot summer day. The castle is pleasant.

I'm so lost in the shimmering beauty of the crystal wall I don't hear or smell the person until I feel a hand curl around my hip. My entire body goes rigid as they lean in, their hot breath tickling over my ear.

"You are most beautiful, Lady of the Mountain. I watched you flying. You are—"

My elbow snaps back, cracking against Inchel's cheek. His head whips back, and I spin, shifting my nails with a thought, raking my talons down his chest. He hisses in pain, but my momentum carries me too far, and I stumble over my human feet. Widening my stance, I lift my leg to knee him in the balls, but he blocks it and slams his arm across my throat, pinning my back to the wall.

My head thunks into the crystal as Inchel growls in my face. "How dare you!"

I shove against him, but my human form is unfamiliar and awkward. I squirm but remain pinned. *Argh! I HATE being human!* Pinning him with a glare, I snarl, "I don't like to be touched uninvited."

His free hand wraps back around my hip, and he steps further into my space. He smells wrong, even to my weak human nose—like decaying leaves and sour almonds. "I will be your King soon."

My talons dig into his forearm that's pressed into my neck. Blood drips down his arm, the red clashing with the bright green scales that have covered him from wrist to shoulder. Our scales and human skin are nearly impenetrable, only able to be pierced by dragon claws or teeth.

I grin, gripping his arm even tighter, but my smile falls and my stomach pitches as he leans in. My claws sink deeper, but he ignores it, slicking his tongue up my neck. I'm so startled, I freeze.

His voice rumbles. "You are a beauty. You will be the one to bring the Mountain clan back into the fold once I am King— once I make you my consort."

Oh, fuck no!

He leans in, dragging his nose up my neck. I rip my talons from his arm and grab his thumb. Wrenching down, I pull until I hear a crack.

"Ahh!" He shoves away from me, cradling his hand against his chest. "You broke my hand!"

I push away from the wall, straightening my dress, wiping his foul saliva from my neck. "Just your thumb. Don't be dramatic."

I may feel clumsy in my human form, but I can still move fast. My hand is around his neck in a flash, and his eyes go wide as my talon-tipped fingers dig into the pulse pounding below his jaw. My hand shakes in rage as I say, "If you touch me again, I'll kill you and save the King the trouble." His lips pull back in anger, his sharp teeth snapping, but I dig my claws deeper, and blood drips down his neck. "And I'd rather die than become your consort."

With a little squelching sound, I rip my talons from his flesh. I grin as a stronger flow of blood pours down his neck, staining his immaculate shirt. He growls at me, pressing his hand to the punctures, but he lets me walk by without another word.

The wounds will close fast enough, especially if he finds a healer, but then he'd have to explain his injuries. I'm sure he'll try to enact some kind of revenge, but satisfaction squares my shoulders as I pass into a large, open library.

I'll be gone tomorrow. Inchel seems to be under the illusion that I will return for the Challenge, but I have no intention of ever setting foot or claw back in this valley or this castle. Inchel can find someone else to torment ... until the King kills him ... hopefully.

I swallow hard, not quite understanding the rush of churning fear that burns through my stomach. I definitely don't want Inchel to take the throne, but it's the thought of Kemremir dying that threatens to drop me to my knees.

My brows scrunch together as I grip the back of a soft leather chair. My head turns as a woman with lavender hair pulled back in a high tail comes into the library with a large vase in her arms. Pure white flowers spill over the lip of the vase, and she sets it in the center of a polished wood table. I take a moment to breathe deeply, inhaling the intoxicating smell of books. This is my favorite room so far.

I clear my throat. "Excuse me."

The lavender-haired woman turns, clasping her hands in

front of her when she sees me, bowing slightly. "Yes, my Lady?"

"I'm"—I look around—"I'm supposed to have dinner with the King. I'm afraid he didn't say where I should go." Tugging at my simple cream dress, the hem swirls around my knees. It's pretty, but seems too simple for dinner with the King. "I'm not sure I'm properly dressed, either."

The woman smiles brightly. "I'll escort you, my Lady. Dinner has been prepared and will be brought up to the King's quarters shortly." She turns to leave the library and smiles at me over her shoulder. "And I'm sure you're dressed fine, my Lady. The King rarely stands on formality."

My fingers pinch and twist at the soft fabric of my dress. I am to eat with the King in *his chambers?* The woman must catch my nervous gesture, because she pauses, placing a hand on my shoulder. Her touch is warm and comforting, like I imagine a mother's touch would be. Though, I wouldn't know.

"I think we can find something if you'd prefer to change."

My lungs fill with a deep breath, and I nod on a slow exhale. "Thank you. I just ..."

Her kind voice fills the silence. "Of course, my Lady. I understand."

"It's Tatha."

"Tatha, my Lady. My name is Fynola."

"Nice to meet you, Fynola."

She leads the way down hall after hall. We pass so many rooms, I can't fathom what most of them are used for. Some are open to my curious eyes, and some are closed, their heavy carved wood doors hiding their secrets from me. Fynola's hips sway within her tight pants that hold her crisp white shirt neatly tucked in. She leads the way up a wide staircase, then down another long hall, this one covered with a plush rug. I have the sudden urge to kick off my boots and wiggle my toes in the deep pile, but I follow along until she finally turns into an open room. As I cross the threshold, I blink a few times as the torchlight from the hall dims and the dark room beyond greets me. It's all shadows and darkness, and my blinking intensifies, and I shake my head to clear my eyes before remembering my night vision doesn't exist in this form.

Fynola glows for a second before bending over and breathing gently into a fireplace. Her dragon's fire spills from her lips and catches on the logs, brightening and warming the room. I blink a few more times as I look around. I'm … confused.

She chuckles, scurrying around the room, pulling a dress from one rack before draping two more over her arm from another rack along the opposite wall. "This is the guest wardrobe. Dragons are notorious for showing up unprepared."

Her laugh is like a bell, and I smile. There are racks and racks of colorful clothes lining two entire walls of this large room. There are dresses, skirts, tops, pants, shorts, and cloaks. I ache to trail my hands down the lines of clothes to caress the velvet, silk, linen, wool, and a few fabrics I can't identify on sight.

I turn a circle. There's a long cream velvet sofa flanked by two blue velvet chairs in the center of the room. I fold to sit on a chair, but pause, hovering over the luxurious seat. Inchel's blood is still on my hands. Ugh. I'm a mess. I'm in no shape to dine with the King.

A cloth slides into view over my clenched hands. I look up at Fynola's smiling face. "For the … blood, my Lady."

She doesn't ask what happened; she simply presses the damp cloth into my hands and crosses the room, shoving aside a tall rack of dresses to reveal a door. Pushing it open, she pulls out an empty rack and rolls it toward me as I wipe my hands clean.

She hangs four dresses on the rack, then turns to me. "We can start with these, and if they don't please my Lady, I'll bring more."

I toe off my boots before walking barefoot to the rack. The first dress is a floor-length velvet of midnight blue with delicate silver embroidery along the hemline. It's beautiful, but a bit much—maybe not for the King, but for me. My fingers pause at the second dress. It's black, like Kem's shadows. There are thin straps that lead to a body-hugging silhouette that would stop mid-thigh. A sheer smoky gray fabric drapes and swirls from the shoulder to just below the hem, softening the tight fit. It's simple, but elegant.

The woman reaches over me and slips the dress from its hanger. "This one, then?"

I nod, speechless, as I pull my shift over my head. She hands me the new dress, and it's even silkier than I imagined as I slip it on. The dress I wore here is plain and soft, but still uncomfortable. Clothes in general seem frivolous, unnatural, and confining. But this dress—I turn, looking at my reflection over my shoulder—might convert me. It hugs my body without feeling constricting, and flows around me like water ... no, like shadows. It's perfect, and my palms start sweating when I think of the King seeing me in this dress.

Fynola reappears with a pair of slip-on flats. At first, I think they are black as well, but when I bend down to slip them on, I notice they're a deep purple, accenting my own amethyst coloring.

"Would you like any jewelry, my Lady?"

The dress and shoes are already overwhelming. Adding more would be ...

She chuckles and moves toward the door. "That's a no then."

I'm not sure what she saw on my face, but apparently, my expression told her everything she needed to know. I follow her back down the hall, but instead of descending the stairs, we turn right. Large oil paintings line this hall. I keep pace, but catch a glance of each piece of art as I pass. They are depictions of the regions of The Crimson Plains. There's the western sea, the crashing waves practically spraying off the canvas. This one shows the ancient forest of the eastern continent. The valley with the castle nestled at its edge is lovely, but doesn't quite catch the magnificence of the real thing. I almost pause as the snow-capped peaks of my mountain range glow at me from the next canvas. A pang of homesickness hits me, churning through my stomach, but I hurry to keep up with my guide.

Fynola stops at the only doors along this long hall. They are open, and she waves me inside. "Enjoy your dinner, my Lady."

I take a deep breath, once again annoyed that it seems shallow compared to the capacity of my dragon's lungs. Stepping into the room, I'm greeted by soft torchlight and a crackling fire in a hearth. The ceiling soars above my head, the room large enough I think Kem and I could both shift and still fit in his room. I swallow at the thought of our dragons in this room ... alone. But then I catch the scent of food—cooked food. Under the char, there is spice. My tongue flicks out with interest before I remember I can't taste the air in this form.

"You look lovely, but I hope you didn't feel you had to change on my account."

Kem's deep voice pools low in my belly, and I turn to find him standing on the far side of the room behind a small iron table set for two. I swallow again and walk forward, looking him up and down.

I smile. "Well, you changed, so it seems the small effort was the correct one."

He glances down, running his free hand over the front of his sleeveless white tunic. His pants are a dark gray and form fitting.

He is ... impressive.

His other hand holds a crystal glass of dark wine, and the liquid swirls with his movement. "Yes, well, I went for a swim, so ..." He leans over, his arms flexing with a casual grace as he grabs another glass, holding it out to me. "Wine?"

I'd prefer whiskey, but I'm not about to turn down the King. I approach the table, reaching out. Right before my fingers wrap around the glass, his scent of leather, cardamon, and vanilla slams up my nose and down my throat. My stomach clenches, and the edges of my vision go a little hazy.

A crash snaps my attention away from the dizzying sensation. I catch the sparkle of broken glass and wine dripping over the edge of the table before I'm slammed against the floor-to-ceiling window.

How did I end up on the complete opposite side of the table?

Kem's large hands press my shoulders to the cold glass. This is the second time tonight I've been manhandled, but unlike with Inchel, I have absolutely no desire to break out of Kem's hold even though there is an ember of violence in his eyes as they rake over my face and down my neck.

His chest rumbles against mine in a low growl. "Why do you smell like him?"

5

KEMREMIR

My BODY TREMBLES with rage and need. The smell of Inchel on Tatha's skin is drawing my dragon dangerously close to the surface. She tilts her head back, and her sparkling purple eyes search mine. I press closer to her, well aware my hard cock is pressing into her stomach.

"Tatha. Why is Inchel's scent on you?"

Her breasts press against my chest with her next breath, and her luscious lips part. "He ... um ... well ... earlier, in the hall, he ..."

"Did he hurt you?"

My cock twitches as her laugh floats up around me. "No. The opposite, actually. I elbowed his face and broke his thumb. He was being ... too familiar, but I set him straight."

Too familiar? My blood rushes through my head, my dragon calling for blood. Hell, *I* want blood. How dare he touch what is mine? I lean into her, running my nose up her neck, and my fingers grip her tighter. It smells like ... he licked her?

My tongue darts out, and I almost gag at the sour taste of his saliva on her skin. But Tatha's shiver encourages me, and I lick her again. My growl gets louder. This time my tongue laps up her taste, free of Inchel's foul essence. She is spice, and earth, and fire—-not smoke, but the sharp undefinable scent of a spark the moment before it catches.

My tongue strokes up the column of her neck and flicks behind her ear. Her moan is like the sweetest melody, and her little body presses harder into mine. My lips brush against her ear. "'Set me straight' if I'm being too familiar."

I nip her earlobe, and she gasps as her nails shift to talons, the sharp points digging into my waist. It's the sweetest pain as she pants, "Kem, I don't understand."

My lips trail back across her neck, and my teeth scrape over her pulse. Her hips buck forward, and I grind into her. "Breath me in, Heilsi. Feel me. Taste me." My lips leave her neck to hover over her mouth. "Kiss me and know. Kiss me and understand."

Her vibrant eyes dance between mine, then our lips crash together, her talons raking through my locs, the tie coming undone as she holds me tight. My chest vibrates with the soul-deep growl that rises from the deepest part of me. My tongue shoves between her lips. Our teeth clash and her tongue dances with mine. I wrap my hand around her thigh, hiking her leg over my hip. I need her closer. Her other leg hooks around me, and her dress bunches up just shy of her sweet center.

Her hips roll, pressing her heat against my cock, her pussy already soaked through her panties. She smells divine, and saliva pools in my mouth.

Her lips rip from mine, her breath panting, pushing her

breasts even higher in the form-fitting dress. "Kem." Her eyes are wide, her lips red from the scratch of my beard. "You are ... We are ..."

MINE!

Jerking my hips forward, I rub my cock against her clit through our clothes. "Say it."

Her head falls back, pressing to the window. I squeeze the soft flesh of her ass as I grip her hair with my other hand, angling her head back even further. She's glorious with her neck exposed to me, but I resist.

Not yet.

Her hips roll against me as she moans under my grip. I lean into her, my breath fanning the little wisps of her hair away from her face. "Say it, Tatha."

Her eyes stay on mine, but her hand snakes between us. Her fingers quickly undo my pants, and my cock springs free. My dragon roars when her hand wraps around me, stroking once. Fuck! I barely keep myself from sinking my teeth into her neck ... barely. I feel her use her thumb to slide her panties to the side, and then she presses the head of my cock to her wet entrance.

No. Not yet. My dragon wants to hear the words. *I* want to hear the words.

I release her hair to grab her wrist; the grip bruising. My cock weeps pre-cum as I pull her hand away from my shaft and stretch her arm over her head. I grab her other arm from where she's gripping my shoulder, and with both her wrists cuffed in one hand, I pin her arms to the window. The position presses her breasts toward me, her hard nipples straining against her dress.

She moans, the sound both aroused and frustrated as she tries to press her hips forward and sink herself onto me. Fuck, how I want to be balls deep in her right now, but I need to hear it. I need her to admit what we are. Out loud. I wish she'd roar it to the heavens, but I'll take a mumbled whisper at this point.

My teeth find her pulse again. I feel her blood coursing through her veins right under my lips. I nip her, and she cries out, her hips jerking forward. She growls, her body vibrating against mine, and I answer with a deeper growl. "Say it."

"Mates! You're my Mate!"

Fuck!

My teeth sink into her neck as I slam my cock deep inside her. She gasps as I stretch her mercilessly. Her sweet blood pours over my tongue, and I drink her down. With her next exhale, she relaxes slightly around my size, and her pussy clenches my cock as I pound into her once, twice.

The sharp prick of teeth penetrates the skin of my chest. My entire body tingles with pleasure. I throw my head back as she licks at the blood staining my clothes and dripping down my torso from where she bit me right through my shirt. I pump into her; her wet cunt sucking me deep. "Mine!"

"Yes! Yours!"

Releasing her wrists, my hands grip her ass as I spin us away from the window. Our dinner forgotten, I stride across the room, through the double doors to my bedroom. Her teeth sink into my neck, and I almost stumble.

"Fuck, Tatha!"

Her face pulls back, and she smiles up at me, her lips stained with my blood. "Yes, please, Mate."

We tumble to the bed, and I catch myself on my forearms to keep my weight from crushing her. My gaze travels from her amethyst hair to her small feet, one of which is missing a shoe. As my eyes climb back to her face, I curl my talon under the neckline of her dress. It's a beautiful dress, but it has to go. "I want to spend hours worshiping you ... later." In one swift move, my claw slices all the way down her dress, the loud tearing sound mingling with her gasp. "But right now, I'm going to fuck you."

"Yes! Kem, my dragon is so close to the edge. I—"

My lips wrap around one pink nipple, and she screams, her body arching off the bed. My teeth scrape across the tight bud before I suck the other in my mouth.

"Kem. Please."

I pull off her with a pop, standing at the edge of the bed. My shoulders bunch as I rip my tunic over my head, tearing the seams in my haste. As I kick my pants off, my eyes burn across her skin as she shrugs out of the scraps of her dress, kicks off the other shoe, and wiggles out of her panties. I kneel on the bed and dive for her mouth. Our kiss is urgent, frantic, and sears right to my soul. With one thrust, I'm hilt deep in her once again, and I roll my pelvis against her clit. Her cry of pleasure fills the room, and I slam into her over and over. Her wet heat sucks me hard and holds me tight within her. With every slap of our sweat-slicked skin, a thread forms between us, pulling tighter and tighter as if our very souls are weaving together.

She bits my lip, and I growl into her mouth. My cock rubs against her inner walls with every thrust, and my lips trail back to her neck where that foul male dared leave his scent, his saliva.

Mine!

My teeth sink back into her flesh, this bite gentler than the first, but no less stimulating. Pleasure pools low in my stomach, and tingling sparks flare in my lower back, shooting up my spine.

"Kem. I'm close. Oh, gods. Kem!"

"Say it, Tatha. Say it, my Heilsi."

"Yours. I'm yours. Mate. Please, Mate. Please. Please. Please."

I lick the bite marks on her skin and whisper against her cheek. "Come for me, Heilsi. Shatter around me. Squeeze me with your perfect cunt. Show me you belong to me as I belong to you."

"Yes! Fuck! Fuck! Oh. Oh. Oh."

Her walls convulse around my cock, and her mouth opens in a silent scream as she comes. The sight of my Mate coming undone under me, the feel of her shuddering around me as she comes apart for me, drives me over the edge.

I drive deep within her as my orgasm tears through me. My body explodes, and the feeling transcends even a free fall from the highest air currents where the air is so thin, it makes you lightheaded.

This is infinitely better. This is ... destiny connecting me with my Mate and her with me.

As the bliss mellows to a sweet thrum of pleasure, and my heart slows from its galloping pace, I gaze down at Tatha.

Her hair is wild around her face. Pleasure glazes her eyes, and little pants of air pass her lips as she tries to catch her breath. I caress her cheek, my talons gone so I can feel her against my fingers. Her skin is so soft, but there's strength behind all that softness.

She stares at my face, and I smile down at her. "My Heilsi. My miracle."

"What does that mean?"

I kiss her lips, and she melts under me. "Fierce one."

She sighs, the sound content. "I can't believe ... why didn't I recognize you earlier?"

My hands continue to trail over her body, tracing and learning every curve and dip. "I think your human form was a bit ... overwhelmed."

Her teeth chew at her bottom lip. "I guess that makes sense." A flush is building once again across the swell of her breasts as my fingers lightly trail over her skin. "What happens now, Kem?"

I smile, ducking my head to trace my tongue around her navel. "Well, first, I need some time to learn my Mate properly." I lick the dip at the top of her thigh. "Then I need to feed my Mate." My teeth nip at the skin of her inner thigh, and her hips lift to meet my lips. "Then I'll bring my Mate back to bed."

"To sleep?"

She chuckles when I raise an eyebrow. "Eventually."

Her fingers thread through my locs, pressing my face between her legs. I laugh, peeking up at her over her gorgeous body. She gasps when she sees I've shifted—just my tongue as it flicks from between my lips. The forked tip tastes the air, catching her scent, her arousal, her fire.

"What's your favorite flower?"

Her head snaps up, confusion crinkling the space between her brows. "Small talk? Right now?"

My tongue flicks her clit. "I told you, I want to learn my Mate."

Her head falls back to the bed. "Fuuuck me. Why do I find that so hot?"

I chuckle against her soaked folds, and her thighs squeeze my head. Pressing a hand to her inner thigh, I spread her open. "So?"

"What?"

"Flower."

"Um." Desperate little breaths push past her perfect lips. I trace a finger down her thigh, skirting around her sensitive flesh. "I can't ... oh, yes, that feels so good ... um ... flower, um, nesaea?"

I stop my teasing touch, looking at her. She lifts her head, meeting my gaze. "What?"

"You surprise me, Tatha. Such an obscure flower. Why that one?"

She wiggles under me, and my fingers dig into the heated flesh of her thigh.

"Kem. *Please*, Mate."

My eyes narrow, and my cock twitches. "Fighting dirty won't get you what you want."

Her hand glides up her stomach and over her breast before her delicate fingers pinch her tight nipple. "What will, *Mate*?"

"Wicked woman. Answers."

Her free hand cups her other breast. "I like that it only blooms for two weeks, and only after the first heat wave of the year. It's small; unassuming with its white petals. It doesn't even have a smell."

I press her thighs wider, blowing heated air over her clenching pussy. "Until it dies."

Her fingers tighten around her nipple as her back arches off the bed. "Yes. Its light honey scent lasts one day, and then it's gone. Makes you appreciate it every year."

I like this answer. I like my Mate.

My tongue curls around her clit before I close my lips over the bud. My fire rises and rushes through me as I swallow her down.

Her breaths pick up speed until she's panting again. I purr as her hands grip my locs tighter, pulling my face into her grinding heat. She's sweet and salty and spicy ... and all mine. I thrust my tongue deep inside her, the forked end curling and tasting every facet of her inner walls.

She moans, rolling her hips against my face, grinding her clit against my beard. I want to carry the taste of her on my face for the rest of my days. My tongue flexes up, caressing the rougher patch of wet flesh that holds her pleasure center. Her pussy clenches around my tongue, and I growl, letting the vibration carry all the way up my throat and down my tongue.

"Fuck, Kem!"

I slide out of her, licking my lips as I pull out of her grip. "Not yet, Heilsi." Her hands fist the bed covers as I trail kisses and gentle bites across her thighs. "How old were you when you got into your first fight?"

Sharp pain stings across my scalp as she yanks on my locs. "Kemremir!"

Reaching back, I untangle her hands from my hair so I can move down her body. "You'll find, Mate, that I quite enjoy anticipation"—My fingers caress the sensitive flesh behind her knees—"the buildup"—My palms caress her skin as I move lower to massage her calves—"Edging." I reach up, sliding a finger down her dripping slit before sinking into her. Pumping once, she moans, but I immediately pull out of her, skimming my wet finger back down her leg. "So ...?"

Her hands fall to the bed, fisting the sheets again. "I was twelve. I overheard someone say my brother was a traitor for leaving the Mountain and shunning our ways." I keep massaging her lower legs, forcing myself to concentrate on her words instead of her creamy skin. "My brother had his reasons for leaving, and while I didn't understand why he abandoned us, I wouldn't abide anyone talking bad about him."

Leaning down, unable to resist any longer, I kiss her ankles, then press my thumbs to the bottoms of her feet, and she moans into the pressure. "What did you do, Heilsi?"

"I launched into him without warning." Her chuckle settles in my heart. "He was over a head taller than me, but even at that young age, I knew how to use my body. It was such a long time ago." A wistfulness carries through her voice.

"And I don't recall much of the fight. I just remember claws, teeth, and blood. The man's friend ended up ripping me off him and dragging me to my father. He took away my books for two weeks, saying I needed to control my temper and learn when and where to channel my anger."

Amazement stalls my breath. The gods have blessed me with this fiery woman. "And have you?"

"Have I what?"

"Tamed your temper?"

She springs up, leaping on me, wrapping her legs around my waist. Reaching between us, her hand wraps around my cock, lining us up, then slowly sinking herself down my shaft. "No."

A powerful possessive force tightens around my heart, and I know I'll use the mystery of my existence to protect Tatha to my last breath. My unusually large size will shield her. My shadows will cloak her from danger. My molten fire will defend her.

I snake an arm around her waist, pulling her against my chest, holding her chin with my other hand, forcing her to meet my gaze. "Good."

Driving into her, she meets every thrust with a beautiful rock of her hips. Her little whimpers drive me on, and I nuzzle her neck. My forked tongue slides up her pulsing vein, her taste searing into my very soul. She's panting so beautifully as she arches back, exposing more of her neck to me.

I mumble into her skin, "So beautiful."

Working my way across her jaw, I nip her bottom lip before taking her mouth in a languid kiss. I release her face to thread my hand between us, finding her clit. Circling it slowly, she moans into my mouth, and when I roll her bud a little harder, her moan cuts off with a little gasp. My thumb presses against her clit, and I hold it there. She tries to pry her lips from mine, but I kiss her deeper. When her breath stalls, I know I've got her on the edge, and this time, I allow her to fall.

Pinching her clit, I alternate grinding my hips into her and savagely thrusting my cock into her clenching pussy. I watch in awe as she throws her head back with a choked roar, her dragon's voice erupting from her with her orgasm.

I keep my eyes on her face, watching every expression as she rides the pleasure and slowly comes down. Her pussy continues to flex around me with her aftershocks, and when her eyes refocus, she looks at me with a dazed expression.

I nod. "That's two. Let's make it five."

Pulling out of her, I press her back into the bed. I rub a finger through her folds, gathering her wetness before bringing my fingers to her nipples and smearing her cream over the sensitive buds. She cries out, thrashing her head to the side. "Kem, it's too much! Oh gods. Too much."

I release her nipple, but continue to circle it slowly. "You can take it, yes, my Heilsi?"

She bites her lip, but nods.

"Good girl." I slide a finger into her pussy, and she lets out a slow breath. I curl a second finger inside her and pump slowly.

Even if that worm, Inchel, hadn't Challenged me, he'd still die at my hands for touching Tatha. I'm going to enjoy tearing him apart. I'm going to bathe in his blood, then I'm going to fuck my Mate amongst the stars as we fall to the earth.

I slide in a third finger, and my thumb gently circles her clit. She's close, and my entire being yearns to see her fall apart again and again and again.

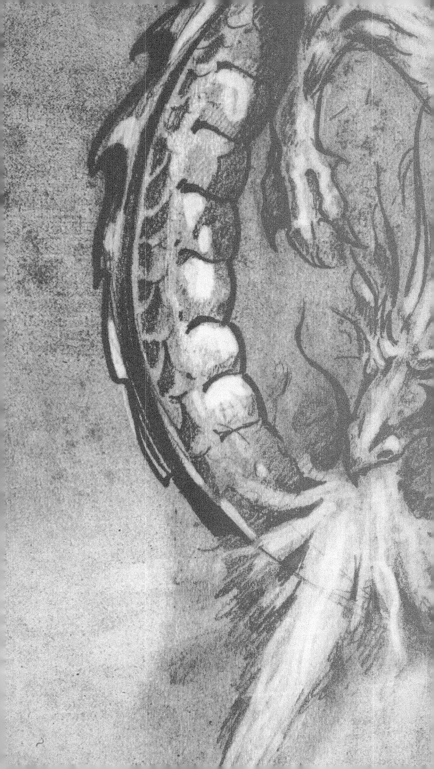

6

TATHA

I'VE LOST count of how many times Kem has made me come—peppering me with questions between earth-shattering orgasms—but I'm pretty sure it's more than the five he promised. I never dreamed my small, little human form could feel so good, so powerful, so free.

And kissing! That's something our dragons can't do, and I'm pretty sure Kem's kisses could tempt me to stay in my human form indefinitely.

Kem kneels between my legs, his muscled, sweaty body looming large over mine. His hands press to the inside of my legs, holding me open to him as he pumps slowly in and out of my swollen pussy. It's like a fever dream. My body responds to him with no thought or effort from me. Every nerve ending is sensitive, like the sharp scrape you feel on your skin before a lightning strike.

I can't believe this is real. I found my Mate.

My hips lift into Kem's languid thrusts, and as my body sinks back into the bed, I go boneless. I don't know when my eyes slid closed, but a small breath puffs from my lips when Kem's arms scoop under my back, his touch caressing my too-sensitive skin. He pulls me against his chest, kissing the top of my head as he slides out of me.

I feel us leave the bed, and his bare feet quietly pad against the floor. There's a squeak of a turning knob, then the splash of water. The air around us grows warm, and then a hot spray of water hits my back, relaxing me even more. I sigh, as Kem steps further under the water, still holding me. He guides my head back, slicking the water over my hair. I keep my eyes closed, mainly because it seems like too much of an effort to try to open them, but also the feel of the water cascading over my skin and Kem's gentle touch is turning my bones to liquid fire.

His lips press to the top of my head again, then my ass meets stone, and Kem presses my back to the wall. I sigh again as I sit propped on what I assume is a built-in seat or ledge. Kem's hands slide over my skin, slippery with soap. When I'm clean, he washes my hair, taking extra care to rinse it, his fingers massaging my scalp, drawing deep moans from my throat.

His chuckle curls through my core, and I'm amazed my body can still respond with such rushing arousal. I suspect it always will—for him, for my Mate.

As younglings, we all learn of fated Mates, and if we're lucky, we might know one or two people in our lives who find theirs. Never did I dream it would feel like this. It's all-consuming. Never did I think I'd find my Mate. And he's the King.

The water shuts off with another squeak of the knob, and then a fluffy towel wraps around my body and I'm being lifted again. I expect the bed, but the surface where Kem lays me is firmer and narrow. I crack my eyes open, noticing I'm on a small sofa.

"I'll have you back in my bed soon enough, Heilsi. I just want to change the sheets."

His fingers linger on my arm, like his body physically doesn't want to leave mine. My eyes slide closed again as I listen to the whoosh and swish of the sheets.

I jerk awake as Kem hooks his arm under my legs and behind my back. "It's okay. Sleep, Heilsi." I sink into the fresh sheets, burrowing my face into the pillow under my head as Kem's voice floats through my exhausted brain. "Rest. We have a long flight to the Mountains in the morning."

I shift, snuggling into a different part of the pillow. My body rolls, flipping to my other side to rub my cheek against this side of the pillow.

"What's wrong?"

My eyes open, taking in his beautiful body, his eyes crinkled slightly with worry. His hand strokes down my arm, and I don't think he even realizes he's doing it. For some unknown reason, my throat burns, and my vision blurs as tears fill my eyes and spill down my cheeks.

Wait. I'm crying? I never cry. I didn't even cry when my mother died. I came close when my father told me he was done fighting and ready for his Elevation, but even then, the tears never came. Yet here I am with salty tears rolling down my face.

Kem's fingers brush against my cheek as he lays down next to me, scooting close to press little kisses to my nose, between my eyes, my forehead. "Tell me. Did I hurt you?"

I'm quick to shake my head. "No! It was w ... wonderful. Beau ... tiful. Maybe a b ... bit overwhelming, but no. I do ... don't know what's go ... going on." My face presses harder into the pillow before I shove it away and plant my face into the sheets, breathing deep.

"Ah, I see."

The bed shifts as Kem gets up, and the tears fall faster. *What the fuck is going on with me?* The bed sinks again, then Kem grabs the pillow over my head. I peel my face away from the sheets, and my brows furrow as he takes the cover off the pillow and puts the old one back on. He holds it out, pressing it to my chest, and my arms wrap around it.

Immediately, the tears stop, and I sigh into the pillow. With my next inhale, I sit up, nearly knocking Kem in the nose with my head. "Are you fucking kidding me?"

His laugh is deep and rich, but my shoulders pinch, and my back goes tense. I clutch the pillow, and Kem reaches around it, cupping my face. "I'm not laughing at you, gorgeous. My dragon is just so happy. *I'm* happy. We're newly Mated, and your dragon needs my scent to be calm—as I need yours. Our bodies will always search for the other, but I suspect the intensity will fade as our bond solidifies. We can talk to Syphe and her Mate about it if you'd like."

My breathing has slowed down, and my body is once again relaxed. "Well, this is … embarrassing."

"No, Tatha. It's a beautiful miracle."

I flop onto my side, curling around the pillow. I try to let it go, but my arms literally won't release it. The pillow muffles my words. "I'm not used to needing … anything or anyone."

His fingers comb through my hair, the half-dry strands spilling around his dark skin. "This isn't a weakness. It's a strength, my love. But I understand. Being pulled so emphatically toward someone, like a compulsion, is unsettling. But we will figure it out. Together."

His eyes travel over every inch of my face, and all I see in them is adoration and awe. I'm not sure I'm worthy of such a look, but I suspect I'm looking at him in much the same way. He climbs over me, his still erect cock brushing against my hip and then pressing to my ass as he pulls me close, my back to his chest.

I press into him, but his hand grips my hip, holding me still. I tilt my face back to look at him, whispering, "Kem, you're ..."

His lips press to my shoulder. "It'll subside. Or maybe not." The kiss turns to a little nip of teeth as he chuckles. "I suspect I'll always want you, and with our bond so new ... but it's fine. You're tired."

I roll over, able to let go of the pillow to inhale his scent right from the source. "What's your favorite flower?"

He chuckles, rubbing his hand down my back. "I've never had one. I collect flora from all over the universe, but have never had a favorite ... until now."

I peer up at him, lips parted, waiting for his answer. He ducks his head, stealing a little kiss before whispering, "The Allium."

My brows furrow, and his finger smooths between my eyes. "It's a flower from the world of Sycame. When they bloom, the pointed petals span larger than my hand. Their pistils glow with brilliant blue iridescence."

"Sounds beautiful."

"They are. I have two in the south solarium. I'll show you sometime."

My jaw cracks with a yawn. "So, why that flower? Why now?"

"Because it smells like earthy cinnamon ... like you."

Scooting up his body, I press my lips against his before snuggling into his chest. "If there was a flower that smelled like you, it would be my new favorite too."

He squeezes me, pressing a kiss to the top of my head. "Go to sleep, Tatha."

Like his words are a command, my body floats into the gray space of sleep, and Kem's burning ember eyes are there to greet me in my dreams.

THE LATE MORNING sun shines brightly behind my eyelids, and after I peel my face from the pillow, I slip from Kem's arms and into one of his shirts. He rolls over, his eyes trailing from my head to my toes and back again. He licks his lips with a wicked smile. "Good morning, Mate."

I press my thighs together to keep the sudden wetness from dipping down my legs. His deep chuckle almost buckles my knees, but then a loud knock on the door makes me nearly jump out of my skin. I'm so startled, scales erupt across my skin, and I barely manage to melt them away before Kem calls out. "One moment."

Crossing to me, he bends down and presses a kiss to my temple, then pulls a shirt over his head. My mouth waters as his hips rock side-to-side while he pulls his pants over his naked ass.

Mmmm. No underwear. Easy access.

I follow him from the bedroom into the large sitting area. Someone has cleared the dinner we didn't eat last night, and fresh breakfast is in its place. He picks out a piece of melon and presses it between my lips. The sweet juice slides over my tongue, and I lick my lips, catching Kem's fingers before he pulls away.

"Wicked woman." He presses his lips to mine, then whispers against my mouth. "I need to get you home to your father, but now all I can think about is that sinful mouth wrapped around my cock."

I swallow, a slow smile spreading across my face. "I can be fast."

His eyebrow lifts, but his eyes go dark. "I'm sure. Problem is, I don't want you fast. I want to savor the feel of my cock sliding down your throat."

I swallow again, and with a deep breath, I walk around him and place a few pieces of melon, two strips of crispy meat, and some flat sweet bread on a plate. Kem crosses to me, lifting the meat from my plate and holding it before my lips. "I know the scent seems off, but trust me."

I crinkle my nose, but obediently open my lips. Fat and salt coat my mouth, then pepper, garlic, onion, and a hint of cardamom explodes across my tongue. My taste buds are different in this form, and the meat is ... delicious.

Kem chuckles as my eyes go wide. I chew slowly, savoring the complex flavors I'd never pick up as my dragon. His lips press to mine, licking the grease from my mouth before presenting me with another bite.

When that piece is gone, he places another strip of meat on my plate before turning toward the doors, calling out, "Enter."

Oh, yeah. Someone has been waiting outside while Kem fed me without a care in the world.

My teeth tear into another chunk of the meat as the door pushes open, and a beautiful woman with bronze hair pulled back in intricate braids walks into the room. She stops mid-stride; the door swinging closed behind her. Her wide eyes skip between Kem and me before a knowing smile turns her face from beautiful to stunning. She bows, sending her bronze hair tumbling over her shoulder. "Your Majesty. My Lady."

"Would you like some breakfast, Syphe?"

She stands, shaking her head. So this is Syphe. My eyes dart to her left wrist, and sure enough, a thin cuff rests against her skin. It's made of supple leather that's banded with engraved bronze that matches the color of her hair. The cuff suits her. Her Mate chose well.

I'd love to ask her questions about the Mating bond and all that it means, but there are more important things to tend to—besides, I've just met the woman. I can't just blurt out, *We're Mated. Help!*

She turns to Kem. "I came by to catch you before you left for the mountains." She faces me, bowing again. "I'm sorry to hear about your father. I'm sure his Elevation will be beautiful."

I grab the flatbread before setting the plate down. "Thank you."

Syphe crosses her arms, her toned muscles flexing with the movement. She would be a fun partner to spar with. Her eyes narrow, and smoke curls from her nose and pours out between her lips when she opens her mouth to speak again. "That worm, Inchel, is pulling support from several other council members. He's running his slimy mouth all over the valley, telling everyone within earshot to get ready for change, for a new King. Ass."

She mumbles that last word under her breath, but Kem still catches it and chuckles. "Let him talk. His death will be that much more of a humiliation to his name and will send a message to his supporters. Are any of the other council members adding their name to the Challenge?"

I spin to face Kem. "More than one dragon can issue a Challenge at the same time?"

He takes a big bite of meat, the fat coating his lips, making them shine. "Technically, yes, though it hasn't been done in ... centuries. I wouldn't put it past Inchel, though."

Syphe shakes her head. "No. Not yet anyway. Though there's still time."

I set my half-eaten piece of bread on the plate, unable to take another bite around the sour churning sensation in my stomach. I face Kem. "If you are Challenged by multiple dragons, can you bring in support? Could I ...?"

He presses his palm to my lower back, his fingers splaying nearly all the way across. "No, Heilsi. But I can handle myself. Allowing you to fight at my side would certainly give me an unfair advantage." He winks down at me, and a blush heats my cheeks.

Syphe's gaze pings between us, and Kem's grin grows wider. "Syphe, Tatha is my Mate."

Her eyes go wide, and her mouth drops open. "Mates?"

Kem smiles and nods. Syphe shouts with a roar as she launches across the room. Before I realize what's happening, her arms wrap around me, crushing me hard to her chest. She spins us in a small circle, laughing as she squeezes me harder. "Congratulations! Oh! This is wonderful news!"

"Syphe, you're crushing her."

She laughs again, stepping back, but holding onto my shoulders. "She's not so delicate." Then she wraps her arms around Kem, hugging him tight. He pats her back, his eyes on mine, a sweet smile on his lips.

Syphe leaps back, brushing her hands down her tunic, turning to me with hands raised. "I'm so sorry. I forgot how intense the early days are. Early weeks ... well, months, if I'm honest."

My brows pinch in confusion, and Kem comes to my side. His arm snakes around my waist as he leans down. His lips brush my ear. "You were growling, Love."

"I was?" I look at Syphe. "I'm sorry. I didn't even know I did it. I didn't think you were ... I mean –"

She waves a hand. "No. No. My fault." Her hand lands on my shoulder and gives me a little squeeze. "You and I will have a long sit down when you get back. Finally, I can talk about life as a Mate with someone! Oh, how exciting!"

"There aren't any other Mated couples here?"

"Not in the valley, no."

I lean into Kem's touch as he presses a kiss to the top of my head, mumbling, "My miracle."

My blush deepens, but when I glance at Syphe, she smiles wide. I really like her.

She crosses her arms again. "The vote continued last night without you. Three applications passed. They're in your office for your final approval."

Kem nods. "I'll get to them when I return from the Mountain, before the Challenge."

I look up at him, knowing my confusion is playing across my face. He doesn't owe me an explanation, but he gives me one anyway. "I have altered the law forbidding outsiders from entering our realm."

My mouth drops open. We might be too secluded up on the Mountain if our clan wasn't aware of this monumental change.

Kem smiles, brushing my hair down my back. "It's an extensive process, and very few applications get approved. An application must pass a majority vote in the council, then it needs my final approval. And once approved, one of my guards must accompany the visitor both in and off world. I assure you, I am being as safe as possible while allowing this small freedom."

I drop my gaze with a nod. He sounds like he's trying to condone his actions to me. He's King. His word is law. But maybe ...

Lifting my head, I search his face, and that little tug on my heart warms with a knowledge I can't explain. He's lonely. He wants someone to talk to, someone to share his burden if simply just by listening.

I fight to hide the fear that bubbles up my throat. I'm not ready for this.

Before I can find the words of encouragement he's obviously yearning for, the same lavender woman from last night enters the room, bowing low. "Your Majesty, I'm here to collect Lady Tatha at your request."

I look at Kem, and he gently shoves me in the woman's direction. "Fynola is going to provide you with new clothes."

Syphe laughs, her head thrown back. "Did he ruin your clothes last night?" My mouth hangs open, but she just shakes her head. "My Mate sure did a number on my clothes when he first scented me. There were only scraps left."

I glance at Fynola still standing in the doorway, but she's just patiently waiting, no judgment on her serene face. My lips quirk in a smile at Syphe. "The dress I borrowed didn't survive." I turn to Kem. "But I can just wear the dress I wore here. We'll be our dragons soon enough. Finery and clothes mean nothing in the Mountain."

He nods. "If you wish. But the royal wardrobe is at your disposal."

My heart stalls for a moment before kicking into a rapid pace. Turning away from Kem to hide the panic I feel pressing against my ribs, I can't help but feel like I'm fleeing as I follow Fynola's swaying lavender hair out of the room.

Ugh. I'm already failing at being a good Mate.

I follow along the long hall of paintings, but I don't take the time to look at them this time. My fingers clutch the hem of Kem's shirt as I stare at my bare feet striking the marble.

The royal wardrobe is at my disposal. Kem is going to want me to live here. Of course he will. He's the King. He can't very well pick up and move to my Mountain. He's going to expect me to live in his castle. I'm going to be forced to wear my human form. I'm going to be stuffed into clothes every day.

Oh, gods.

My palms are sweating as I enter the large room with all the fine clothes, and the delicious food I had for breakfast turns into a ball of lead in my stomach. Quickly, I pull Kem's shirt over my head and slip my simple dress down my body. I stuff my feet into my boots and turn to Fynola. I force a smile, though it feels tight. "Thank you for your kindness. I think I can find my way back."

She nods. "If you're sure, my Lady."

Rushing from the room, I head back the way I came. My body pulls me down the halls, knowing where Kem is. I think I could find him in a maze with my eyes closed.

Shit. My body misses him. I crave his touch. I yearn for his gaze on my body. I force my feet to slow, though it's a challenge. Can I leave my clan? Can I change who I am for my Mate?

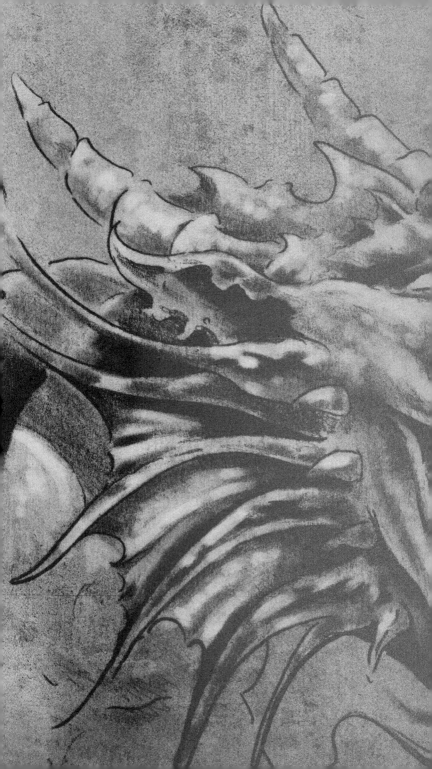

7

_____

KEMREMIR

THE SECOND TATHA'S dragon burst from her skin, my soul sighs and my beast roars. She's glorious. Her vibrant amethyst scales ripple across her compact body, and the occasional gold scale winks in the sunlight. Her claws tear into the ground, and her belly glows with the heat of her inner fire. Sitting back on her muscular haunches, she spreads her wings, reaching the tips wide before flapping them in the gentle breeze.

I'm transfixed. After being inside my Mate last night, my dragon is subdued ... for now.

She stretches her wings, and a strange purring sound vibrates up my throat. Her head tilts in my direction, her gold-ringed purple eyes sparkling down at me. Her dragon's voice is just a hint deeper than her human one with an edge behind it. "What's wrong?"

I shake my head, my locs swaying over my upper back. My

shadows curl out from my skin, engulfing me in darkness before my dragon form tingles across my skin. Stretching my own wings, they double her span. My shadows trail from each wing as I flap them slowly, and a trail of shadows follow the flicking of my tail.

Tatha's eyes are on me, and my chest puffs out at her attention. The purple of her scales deepens with her flush, and her wings fold gracefully along her back. The ground shakes under my feet as I take the few steps to close the distance between us. My head dips, caressing my cheek to hers. Her scent of fire, cinnamon, and earth is stronger, and there's a hint of heavy smoke under it.

My tail wraps around her back leg, and her scales flutter with her shiver. My dragon fire roars through my veins, and curls of smoke plume from my nostrils. We need to get airborne. Now. Before I take her right here in the grass outside the border of the castle gardens.

I shake my head, forcing my tail to unwind from her leg. My tongue flicks out a few times, tasting the air, learning the currents, but I'm nearly overwhelmed by the taste of her scent in my mouth.

Bunching the muscles of my back legs, I spring up, flapping my giant wings in great strokes, my shadows following me into the sky like streamers of smoke.

Tatha releases a feminine growl as she launches up behind me. When I glance back, she's spinning and dancing through the trails of my shadows, and a rumbling laugh tumbles from my chest.

I find a fast moving current that's pulling north, so I set my wings under the tug of the air and glide back and forth. My shadows curl, twist, and flutter in my wake, like they are as eager to dance with Tatha as she is to dance with them. I find myself looking back more and more, ignoring where I'm going to take in the glorious scene behind me.

After a while, Tatha breaks through the smoky trail of my shadows, shooting her small body under mine, then quickly banking right to float up at my side. Her fangs are long, and every lethal, pointed tooth gleams at me when she smiles. My heart stutters at the site, and I go hard with wanting her. My body tilts toward her, and the top of my wing caresses the underside of hers. We stay like that for a moment, and I absorb her warmth, her beauty, her grace, calming my dragon down from the claiming urge.

We've dropped slightly, so I shift away from her and flap my wings in lazy strokes. She pumps her wings to keep up. Every flap of my wings takes two of hers, so I keep my pace moderate. I'm in no rush to end this first flight with my Mate.

We fly for hours, occasionally brushing our wings together as we head north. Her Mountain grows larger as the day dies. The sun paints the snow-capped peaks a deep orange, then a pale pink, followed by a soft lilac that cools to a deep blue.

I fall back, letting her take the lead. She puts a little extra swish to her tail, and I nearly drool at the sight of her swaying hips as she angles between the two highest peaks. Pulling her wings in just slightly, her speed picks up, and she arrows through the twists and turns between the mountains. My jaw clenches as I pull my wings in closer. I'm so much larger than her. This is going to be a tight fit.

Adrenaline courses through me as I keep an eye on the flash of amethyst before me. My body angles hard with every sharp turn, and the wind tears at my scales. I bank left, but cut it too close, and a scraping pain scratches along the top of my rear foot as it drags against snow, ice, and rock. A groan sounds behind me as a small avalanche collapses toward the ground far below.

"Shit!"

The wind carries my curse away as I bank hard to the right, nearly crashing into the mountain as the purple streak of Tatha disappears around another bend.

Finally, I take a deep breath as the space around us opens slightly. She pulls up, slowing her screaming pace. Focusing beyond her, the gigantic carved opening to the Mountain clan's home looms before us. It's been centuries since I've been here, and it's no less awe-inspiring than the last time. Columns carved into the side of the mountain stand ten-dragons tall. Twisting bodies of dragons climb up the stone in intricate carvings. The mouth of the cave—though it feels wrong to call such a place a cave—arches open, and there's two guards posted at the edges of the entrance.

Tatha barks twice, slowing her pace even more. A moment later, the dragon on our right shoots a column of fire that lasts three seconds. I assume that's the signal to proceed, because Tatha dives in a lazy circle until her talons grip the ledge.

She strides far enough in to give me room to land. The sharp crack of rocks breaking free and tumbling down the side of the mountain echo loudly as I touch down. I immediately fold in my wings to keep from hitting the guards. As vast as the entrance is, I'm the largest dragon of all the dragon clans. I don't know if I have my parents to thank for my size and strength, or if the gods blessed me for some reason. Either way, I'm thankful for my unusual prowess. It's helped me take and keep the throne, and now I will use my size and power for the ultimate purpose—protecting my Mate.

The guards lower their heads to the ground as I pass, and I dip my head in acknowledgment. My tongue flicks out, picking up Tatha's taste in the crisp mountain air. I follow her swaying hips and swishing tail deeper into her home.

The smooth rock ceiling towers overhead. The space is so

large, even I could take flight in here comfortably. We move deeper into the cave, and as the fading light of the day dims, flickering torchlight takes its place. From the corner of my eye, I catch the occasional flash of raw gems and crystals embedded in the smooth rock walls. Carvings of dragons decorate the walls as well, the crystals flashing in their eyes and scales as if the artist carved the reliefs around the gems. My front foot drops slightly, and when I glance down, I see I've stepped into a fossilized claw print.

I follow Tatha around a gently turning corner, and a large common space opens before us. A circle of soft moonlight spills onto the floor from a vent shaft high above. Several dragons pause, their movements frozen for a moment as they realize who I am. Each head bows low, and they back away as I pass through the space. I nod at each ... a gray, a sapphire blue, a vibrant red, and a bronze almost identical to Syphe.

When the pale moonlight hits Tatha, her amethyst scales turn blue for a moment and I suck in a deep breath.

She's magnificent.

But my heart squeezes with pain as her head drops as she leads me down a narrow shaft. I can taste her sorrow as we draw closer to where her father must be.

She moves with ease, but no matter how tightly I tuck in my wings, the edges still scrape against the walls. To keep the panic from closing in, I keep my eyes trained on Tatha. The memories of the dark tunnels under the Unseelie castle threaten to close my throat. That day, my goal was to rescue the captured youngling from the dark fae, and Raelyn's younger brother led our rescue mission into the bowels of the tunnels deep underground the Unseelie realm. Things had not ended well.

Panic grips my chest, so to distract myself, I think of that youngling, wondering if Tatha will ever want children. It's too soon to talk of such things, but regardless, the matter is completely out of my hands beyond having a conversation with her about it. Females can hold viable sperm from multiple partners for up to a year, able to sterilize that sperm at any time. Or, she can choose when and from which partner to procreate with. The power lies completely with the females —as it should be.

My wandering thoughts of Tatha's stomach swelling with my young keeps the fear at bay until the tight space opens into another large room. Torchlight flickers around the edges, leaving the center dark, but my dragon sight penetrates the shadows easily. Tatha crosses the room, her head low, her tail dragging behind her, her wings limp. Beautiful paintings of the mountain spread along the floor, and a small pool ripples to our left, fed by the steady drip of water down the wall from somewhere outside.

My snout scrunches as a heavy scent takes over the clean mountain air and dryness of the caves. This new scent even overpowers Tatha's earthy essence.

Sickness. Death.

Tatha drops to her belly. Her tail protectively curls around her as she lays her muzzle on the neck of the sleeping dragon in the large nest along the back wall. I ache to hold her. My claws scrape grooves in the diamond-hard floor as I resist curling my body around hers. I want ... no, I *need* to take her pain away. But I can't. This is something she must endure. But I can be here for her.

Hopefully, that is enough.

I inch closer, slowly lowering myself to the ground.

Tatha rubs her cheek along the dragon's neck. "Father?"

He stirs. Most of his emerald green scales are muted, some completely devoid of color. When his eyes flutter open, I notice his once vibrant eyes are no longer green, but a cloudy white. His body shakes as a cough bubbles from his chest, and when he's able to take a breath, he focuses on his daughter.

"Tatha? Sweet girl. You've come back."

"Of course, father. The King has come."

"Oh, ho!" A bit of life kicks through his voice as he shifts. Tatha moves back, her tail brushing mine. When she moves to pull away, I curl my tail around hers to keep her there. I need the contact as much as I suspect she does. "The great Kemremir has at last come to the Mountain."

I smile at the laughter in his words as I crawl closer. "Of course, old friend. I only wish I had known of your condition earlier."

He shakes his head as he stiffly props his front legs under his chest. "Nothing to be done. You're a busy man, and we here in the Mountain like our solitude." He turns toward Tatha. "How was it being in your human form?"

Her scales darken with a blush, and I smile as she shakes her head. "It was ... interesting."

Tovra's eyes dance between us, and one of his great brows climbs his forehead. "Oh! Well, then." His eyes land on me, and though there's a flicker of joy in the depths of his eyes, he's fixed a stern look on his face. "Are you going to do right by my girl?"

"Father!"

"Well, you're my only daughter."

"We don't need to be discussing this. The King is here for you, father."

Tovra looks between us again, shaking his head. "I know you've had your dalliances, Tatha ..."

At the thought of Tatha with other lovers, a growl rumbles from my chest, and her vibrant scales pale slightly. I shrug, unapologetic of my possessiveness, and just barely resist chuckling at her embarrassment.

"Oh gods, please, father."

Tovra continues, "... but this seems like something more." He turns to me. "Yes?"

I nod, glancing at Tatha. Her blush has deepened, but she doesn't nod or shake her head, just stares at me, so I answer honestly. "Yes, Tovra. Your daughter is my Mate."

Tovra's eyes go round, and a little spark of green flares around the pale edges. "Mates! Oh, my sweet girl, congratulations! And with the King!"

Tatha buries her face between her front legs, hooking her left foot over her eyes.

I laugh. "I am honored to be Tatha's Mate, and yes, I will do right by her. Always."

Tatha lifts her head, her fire burning in the center of her eyes. Tovra nods, his smile widening as he relaxes into his nest. "Aye. You were always an honorable dragon, Kemremir. I am happy for you both. I was content with my fate before, but now I am truly at peace."

Tatha's tail winds higher up mine, and I'm not sure she's aware she's doing it, but my chest purrs at the contact. "With your permission, Clan Leader, I will stay in the Mountain until your passing, and when the time comes, I will light the fires of your Elevation."

Tovra nods, resting his head in the deep blankets and large pillows. "Of course. My King does not need to ask permission. Tatha will see that you are comfortable." He chuckles, and she blushes again. "I feel my soul pulling toward the ether. Your stay should not be long."

A little huff of sorrow slips from Tatha, and I rest my foot on Tovra's. "I will stay as long as necessary."

There's no response. His soft breathing evens out, and his body slips back into sleep. Tatha pulls more blankets and pillows around her father before rising and backing away.

When we reach the edge of the room, her voice whispers over her shoulder. "I'll take you to your room. Unless you're hungry and would like to go on a hunt."

Before she passes into the narrow hall, I move around her, blocking her exit. "I'd love to hunt with you, Tatha, but I will not need my own room. I'm sleeping with you."

The scent of her arousal floods my nose, and I growl, my fangs nipping at her flank as she slips by me and into the tunnel. My body vibrates as I follow her. Her scent is concentrated in this close space, and the swish of her tail becomes violent, and I realize she must have picked up the scent of my desire for her.

The panic-inducing space no longer presses in on me. All I see is her. All I smell is her need. When my body breaks through into the open space of the common room, my wings unfurl with the desire to draw my Mate's attention. But she only smirks at me, the expression fierce. Her head tilts up, and the next second she launches up, spearing through the vent in the ceiling. I eye the opening skeptically, unsure if I will fit. But I will follow my Mate anywhere.

I leap into the air, climbing hard and fast to build my momentum enough so I can tuck in my wings and shoot through the hole in the ceiling. A few scales on my back scrape the rim of the hole, and my heel catches on a rock before I'm able to spread my wings again and drive myself into the star-lit night, chasing the amethyst beauty that's gliding into the light of the full moon.

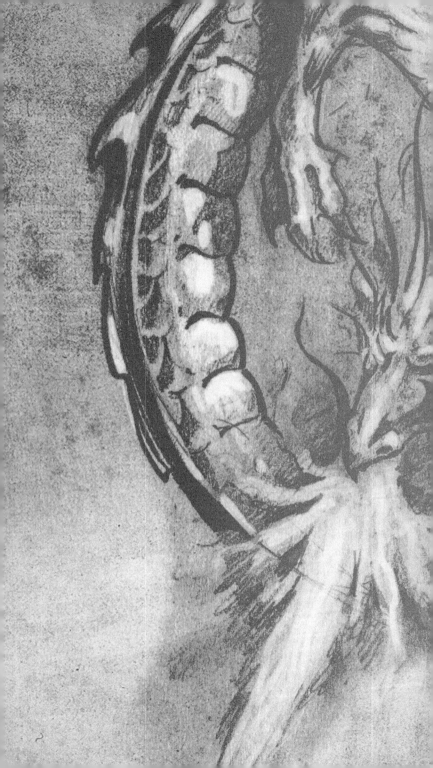

8

TATHA

THE SATISFYING SNAP of bone crunches between my teeth, the marrow coating my throat. But as the hot rush of blood floods through my mouth, and the coppery smell invades my nose, I find myself missing the spice and flavor and even the char of the cooked meat from breakfast. One taste fed to me from Kem's fingers, and I'm hooked.

I glance at the impossibly large black dragon next me. Though, I'm pretty sure my addiction has everything to do with the sexy man, and less about the actual food.

Rolling the bones and flesh around in my mouth, I spit out a curled horn on the ground where I lay. The heat of my inner fire melted the snow when I landed, and my second kill waits for me off to the side.

You wouldn't think it by looking at them, but the shaggy horned tretlac, with their wide-set eyes and soft hooves, are fast beasts. They scamper across the mountainside and leap between crags. I've watched their frantic fleeing all my life, and it still amazes me they don't immediately fall to their deaths.

I glance at Kem again, a long tretlac leg disappearing down his throat as his blood-coated teeth snap and grind his meal. By the time I snatched my two tretlacs, he had killed five. He offered me one of his, but my two are more than enough, and as he finishes off his last one, I hide a small smile. The King is a large beast and just consumed five large tretlacs in one sitting.

Why does that turn me on? Will everything this male does affect me?

Kem's long tongue licks his lips, cleaning the blood from his face, but his eyes pin to me as he dips his head and starts to lick his claws. I'm transfixed as his tongue carefully collects every stray morsel, every tuft of hair, every drop of blood.

Why hasn't he tried to claim my dragon? I've scented his arousal. His eyes speak of his desire for me, but he's done nothing more than brush gentle touches against my scales. Does he not want—

Kem's deep voice snaps me from my spiraling thoughts. "I thank you for the hunt, Tatha. It's been a long time. I'd almost forgotten the rush of the chase. It was most enjoyable."

The sudden thought of him chasing me down plays out in my mind, and my scales heat with my blush.

Kem's giant head tilts to the side. "What delicious thoughts are running through that beautiful head of yours?"

With a shake of my head, I lift my flank, scratching my front claws into the ground as I arch my back in a stretch. I know what this position does to my body, and a swell of satisfaction lights up my body at Kem's purr. "Wicked woman."

I grin, flashing my fangs, then roll over into a fresh patch of snow. It sizzles and melts around me as I clean the blood and viscera from my scales. Kem growl-laughs at me.

I leap into the air. The snow puffs and curls out behind me in the draft of air, and in the next second, Kem is at my side. I brush against him as we fly at a lazy pace back toward my Mountain. A touch of wings, a caress of tails, I even trail my knuckles down his back, but no matter how I play and tease, he doesn't pounce. He doesn't claim my dragon.

The moonlight reflects and shimmers off my scales, and I realize Kem remains a dark blot in the sky. It's as if his shadows consume the light before it touches him.

I wonder ...

Floating to the right, I angle up into a current that takes me above Kem. I fly high, and when I look down, it takes me a full minute to find him. Even as large as he is, his body melts into the shadows of the landscape far below.

Amazing.

I take a gentle dive back down to his side, and he grins at me. "Find what you were looking for up there?"

"Yes, but it took me a while." My tail flicks through his trailing shadows. "That is incredible."

He looks over his shoulder, watching the trailing darkness swirl away from his body. "I suppose."

There's a hard line of resignation to his face, and I realize the mystery of his color and his shadows might be a source of insecurity for the seemingly unflappable King. My heart kicks with a little pang of pain for my Mate, but I shake it off with a smile as I pull close to him, our wings touching again. If he won't claim me, I need something to work off this edge.

"It's only twenty-three miles from here back to the Mountain. Ready?"

He looks at me, and I gasp as the moonlight catches in his eyes. He's a vision of absolute power. I imagine if I could see him beyond my biased Mate bond, I might be a little afraid of him. But all I see is ... my dragon.

I grin, tensing my muscles. "Go!"

With one quick flap of my wings, I take off. His heat is right on my flank, and I fight to find the currents that will give me an edge. Kem may be large and powerful, but I'm quick.

My heart races, the molten fire in my belly smolders as fear and excitement mix with the chase. A sting of pain shoots up my tail, and I realize Kem has nipped me. I'm sure if I looked back, I'd see his wide grin, but I keep my gaze forward, pushing my speed.

I'm breathing hard, and my muscles are beginning to burn as I pump my wings harder and harder. I imagine I can feel Kem's hot breath on my heels, and I take a sharp left, hoping to gain some distance.

I feel more than see him take the turn with ease. How the fuck did he do that? His size should have made that maneuver impossible. Heat curls along my belly as a ball of fire spears past me.

He's playing with me!

The entrance to my home opens up before me, and I spear toward it. A black blur whips past me, and Kem slides to a landing just as I spread my wings and touch down. I raise an eyebrow, frustrated that he's not even breathing hard. I pant a few breaths before saying. "I thought you were going to let me win."

He chuckles, the sound low and rich. "I thought about it." He stalks toward me, completely ignoring the guards standing off to the side. His head dips, and his hot breath whispers across the scales of my cheek. "But I didn't want to give you any illusions as to your fate the next time you run from me." I swallow as his large body rubs along my side. The contrast of his hard scales and warm body sends a shiver down my spine.

"I enjoy the chase, Tatha. But next time, I'll catch you." His tongue licks down my small horns, and I barely hold back a groan. "I'll show all the stars that you are mine as I take you, Mate."

What the fuck is he waiting for?

He steps to the side, and I stand frozen with desire. Kem bows his head, seemingly unaffected, but I can smell his arousal, so I know he must be able to smell mine. I glance at the guards, realizing they can probably smell me as well.

I shove past Kem. "Come on." I stalk into the cave, catching Kem's wink at one of the guards who smiles back at him with a quick bow of his head. "Bastard."

The word is mumbled under my breath, but Kem chuckles behind me, having heard me.

We make our way through my home. A few dragons linger in the common spaces, but most are tucked into their nests for the night. A little flutter of nerves dances through my chest as I make the final turn and cross into my room. It's not as large as my father's, but there's natural light from a vent high overhead. Not only is my floor painted with colorful scenes of the mountain, but the art scrolls and weaves up the walls as well, cocooning me in beauty and color. Silky fabric flutters from the ceiling, swaying in the gentle currents from the vent. The pale blue fabric reminds me of the morning sky, and I smile.

I cross to the side wall, straightening the large scrolls stacked in the beautifully carved nook. Dragons love stories. We love to read, and I love it more than most. But books and dragons don't mix well. It's not the small print—our sharp sight easily makes out each word—it's the pages. Trying to turn tiny fragile paper with sharp claws is nearly impossible. Luckily, there are many well-paid scribes whose only job is to copy stories from books to large scrolls made from thin, flexible metal.

Lifting the last one from the table next to the nook, I press the silver button at the top of the scroll. With a swish, the metallic paper slides into its container. I set it in its place and turn to find Kemremir watching me.

He comes to my side, his voice quiet. "It's lovely. Your book collection is impressive."

"My knees almost buckled when I saw your library at the castle."

Kem chuckles. "If there are any books you wish to have copied to scrolls, just let me know. We have a dedicated scribe on staff."

I immediately start creating a mental list, and Kem's chuckle gets louder. "Uh oh. I think my scribe is going to have her work cut out for her."

My claw clicks against the floor in slight embarrassment, but he nudges me. "Your room is lovely. Thank you for sharing it with me."

I nod, unable to keep the blush from darkening my scales —not that he gave me a choice. When I step away from the nook, I notice my nest is much larger than when I left it. My blush deepens as I realize my father must have arranged for more material to be brought here after he learned Kem is my Mate.

My tail swishes back and forth over the bright paintings as I try to decide what to do. But then Kem strides past me. His snout nuzzles into my nest. His chest expands as he takes a deep inhale, and I go wet as I watch him take in my scent. He turns a tight circle, adjusting the soft blankets and plush pillows as he takes another circle, then another before lowering himself into the nest.

His eyes find mine with an expectant look. I'm drawn to him by a phantom pull from the center of my body. My feet carry me to my Mate, and I step into my nest, inhaling the heady mix of our combined scents in my space. My body both relaxes and hums with arousal.

Kem's voice is soft. "Come, sleep with me, Mate. It's been a long day."

My body obeys him, and I practically flop down, curling into his side. He wraps his body around mine, his warmth seeping into me, his quiet purr vibrating against my back. His tail encircles us, and he tucks me under his chin.

I count his breaths until mine sync with his, and before I know it, I'm slipping into sleep.

THE PAST THREE days have passed in a blur. Kem has stayed at my side almost every moment. The news of our Mate bond traveled fast, and looks and stares followed us everywhere.

I'm used to being looked at for my duo-chrome nature, but this attention ... I don't mind. I'm proud to be Mated, and I'm proud of my Mate. I find myself touching him all the time, and Kem is the same. If it's not our wings brushing, it's our tails twining, or our bodies brushing together. Every caress is comforting and arousing. Each passing day draws our bond tighter.

Still, he has yet to take me in this form. I've come close to just making the move myself—several times—but always lose my nerve. What if he doesn't want me like that as my dragon? What if his desire is tied to my human form, and he's waiting for our shift?

Before him, all I've ever known is the violent, rushed sex of dragons. Having sex in my human form was ... I can't find the words, but every time I think about it, the muscles low in my belly clench, and my scales darken to a deep indigo. I loved it.

It was so different. My body was so sensitive beyond anything my dragon has ever felt.

But my dragon is who I am.

So I've waited and am doing my best to shake off the insecurity bubbling up with each passing day.

Kem and I have passed the days visiting my father, whose remaining vibrant green scales fade more with each passing hour, but Kem has always been there to distract me from my sorrow. He shared tales of the kingdom. He told his story of how he met the Seelie fae royal children. His face softened when he spoke of Raelyn, now the Seelie queen, and I think I'd like to meet this woman.

I shared pieces of my childhood, telling him about my family; of how my mother died when I was four, and though she wasn't my father's Mate, she was his true love, and he never married again. Kem asked about my brother, and while I have fond memories of Kogra, I haven't seen him in over thirty years, and I'm not sure who he is now.

Kem told me stories of my father and him. I had no idea my father was one of Kem's main supporters in his Challenge against Kem's predecessor. My father fought at Kem's side when Ruenar, the former King, sent his fighters to take out Kem before the Challenge. I never knew where the ragged scar on my father's rear right leg came from. Now I do. Kem won the Challenge and granted my father the Mountain territory, allowing my clan to grow and prosper in peace.

I knew the story of the rescue attempt of one of the dragon younglings, but when he told me the story ... when his eyes darkened as he recalled the cave-in, his broken wing, the crushing weight ... the tangy scent of fear I picked up the first time I brought Kem to my father finally made sense. Since then, I've made sure to avoid the smaller passages.

I showed him my favorite routes to fly, where the currents

hold you with little effort, or they scream against your wings, making you fight for every flap. We've hunted, and we've swum in the freezing waters of the lake that's fed by the mountain snows. I've shown him every nook and room in the vast caves I call home, and he curls himself around me every night.

But he hasn't claimed me.

The morning of our fourth day, I'm nudged awake by Kem's snout gently pressing against my neck. His scent of leather, cardamom, and vanilla pulls me from my dreams, but then I burst awake, like breaking the surface of stinging cold water.

"Easy, my Heilsi. It's time. I'm here." Kem's voice tries to soothe me, but I know.

I curl into his warmth and breathe him in for a few moments before I slowly stand. Shaking off the last of my sleep, I duck my head under the small fall of water in the far back corner of my room. Relieving myself, I shiver under the cold spray and close my eyes as I step out, crossing the room. Kem follows without a word, but his silent presence gives me strength.

The second I step into my father's room, I feel his impending death press in on me. His breathing is shallow and all his scales have leached of color. His gray body lays sprawled in his tangled nest, but his eyes slide open and land on me.

I lower my body to the floor and crawl to him. A soft smile curls up his lips, and I notice even his sharp teeth are gray. "My dear daughter. I love you. No matter your path in this life, know I'm proud of you."

I lay my head near his, trying to find his comforting scent under the cloying sickness that clings to this room. "I'm not ready, father."

"No one ever is. But you will be fine, dear girl."

83

I feel Kem behind me, and my father shifts slightly to raise his gaze, though he's not strong enough to lift his head. "I thank you for your time, your Majesty. Your presence is an honor."

"It is I who am honored to be here for you, my friend."

Father's gaze shifts back to me, and I have to crawl closer to hear him. "Your brother is coming." My brows furrow. "He sent word yesterday. He will be here for my Elevation."

I shift on my haunches, trying to recall the exact shade of the yellow of Kogra's scales.

My father's quiet voice disrupts my thoughts. "I know that look, daughter. Kogra didn't abandon you. He didn't abandon us. He had another path he needed to follow. But he is coming home." My father's snout weakly shoves against mine. "I think maybe his experience outside of the clan will bring a much needed perspective to our people. My fear is that our clan is unknowingly suffering in our seclusion." I can't stop the frown that pulls at my lips. "Tatha, your Mate was less than a day's flight from our Mountain." I glance at Kem as my father continues, "This may be the ramblings of an old dragon at the end of his days, but there is so much life out there, we shouldn't ... we *can't* continue to hide away from the world because of past pain."

I blink several times, unable to process this shift in my father. He loves our Mountain. He loves the seclusion, the peace. These caves are all I've ever known—because of him. But he is right, my Mate was right here.

My father chuckles, reading the conflict on my face. "Darling girl, you would be a fantastic clan leader, and if you choose that path, our clan will prosper under your leadership." His eyes flick to Kem before coming back to me. "But I think, if you look within your heart, your happiness lies along a different path."

The floor vibrates as Kem lowers to his belly. "Tovra, whatever your daughter chooses, know I will support her." His tail brushes against mine, and the pressure of my sorrow, my longing, my responsibilities, and my dreams pushes against my ribs. But then it all slides away with Kem's next words. "I will be here for her for the rest of her days."

My father exhales slowly. "And that is all I can ask."

We sit in silence for a while. Father dozes in and out, occasionally speaking with Kem in soft tones, sometimes sharing light-hearted stories about my childhood and all my rebellious antics.

A sound at the entrance draws my gaze, and Kem shifts closer to me as the flash of bright summer-yellow scales passes through the door. I nod at my brother. "Kogra."

"Sister. It's good to see you."

I want to retort that it took father's impending death to bring him home, but I bite my tongue.

Kogra bows to Kem. "Your Majesty. You honor our family with your presence."

Kem's tail strokes down mine, and Kogra's eyes widen. Kem smiles. "Of course. Tovra is a friend. And I am here to support my Mate."

I blush, avoiding Kogra's startled gaze. How easily Kem announces our bond. There's pride in his voice, so why ...

"Son." Father's weak voice silences us. "Welcome home. I am glad to see you one last time, here at the end."

Kem moves aside, but maintains contact with a foot pressed to my side. Kogra crawls forward, pressing his head to father's, tears in his voice. "I'll miss you, father. I should have stayed."

"No, son. You followed your heart. You had to leave to know if you belonged here."

Kogra rubs his face against father's cheek. "I do. This is my

85

home. These are my people." He turns to face Kem. "And I will stand with the King. He will have the support of the Mountain clan at the Challenge and beyond."

A small gasp leaves my lips. I'd almost forgotten about the Challenge.

Kem nods, his foot stroking me slowly, comforting me. "I thank you, Kogra." A quiet chuckle rumbles from his chest. "I imagine an additional show of support from the Mountain clan will rile Inchel."

Father laughs, but it turns into a hacking cough. Once he catches his breath, he closes his eyes. "I wish I could see you tear that worm apart. But I've been present at more than a few of your Challenges over the years, Kemremir. You'll be fine."

Kem's foot strokes my side. "Aye. I'll be fine."

We fall into silence, and an hour passes, then another. The rhythmic drip of the water along the back wall lulls father into a deep sleep, and as I watch, his sides expand, then release one last time. His body goes still, and grief presses in on me like the room just caved in.

I sit there, waiting for him to take another breath, but it never comes.

Kem nudges me with his snout. "Would you like to take him to the crest, or shall I have the guards bring him?"

Kogra and I speak at the same time. "I'll take him."

I lock eyes on my brother, and Kem stands, backing away. Kogra and I carefully work together to lift our father, and we settle him on Kogra's back. I walk at his side, steadying my father's body with my tail.

We leave my father's room, Kem at our backs, guards trailing behind, and I take a deep breath. It's happening. My father is gone. He will be Elevated tonight, and after ... after, I'm going to have to face my future, whatever that looks like.

I glance back at Kem.

9

KEMREMIR

I HAVE SPENT the past four days in near bliss, learning my Mate. But I've also been fighting with myself every moment I'm with her as my dragon.

I want her. I need her. Her dragon calls to mine. Desire has constantly roared through my body, heating my blood and spearing through my cock. I've held back. Every day my human mind argues with my dominant dragon.

I haven't taken a female in my dragon form since I was very young. Sex as a human is much more stimulating. It can be sweet, tender, rough, desperate, leisurely, or fierce. Sensations are different on delicate flesh. Human tastebuds pick up more complex flavors.

But dragons fuck.

We use claws and teeth. We take. We fight. We claim.

I know Tatha has lived as her dragon her entire life, and I'm sure she is a fierce partner in her natural form. But I am a beast of another nature. I'm stronger. My fire is hotter. I'm larger—in all aspects. I'm afraid I'll scare her, or worse. I can't chance hurting her. Eventually, my dragon will win, and I'll take her. But not today.

Today is for remembering my friend, for sending him home to the stars.

Tatha, Korgra, and I step outside. Heavy flakes of snow melt on my scales, and a procession of the dragons of the Mountain follows. I trail my Mate and her brother along a path that winds up the side of the mountain. Clouds have covered the moon, and the wind picks up as we come around a sharp curve. A large open plateau opens before us. With every step, my legs sink deeper into the snow.

Tatha and Kogra's muscles flex as they push through the deep drifts despite their heated bodies melting away a lot of the snow. I rear back, flap my wings once, and leap over them. My spread wings bring me down gently.

"Kem, what—?" The wind steals Tatha's question.

I stop their progress for a moment as I take a deep breath. Gathering my fire, I exhale flames and smoke. My belly glows bright against the dark, snowy night. My head sways left-to-right, then back again. The snow melts and steams, but I don't stop. The soggy ground starts to bubble, then the water evaporates under the heat until dry, hard-packed earth spreads before us.

Stepping to the side, I nod at my Mate, and a sad smile curls up her lips. "Thank you, Kemremir."

My wings flutter at my name on her lips, and I bow my head to her as she and her brother pass. They carry their father to the far ledge where stone juts out beyond the mountainside. Kogra lowers himself to the ground, and Tatha helps him ease Tovra from his back. In tandem, they flank their father's body and sit back on their haunches, curling their tails around their legs. I step forward, and every dragon bows, pressing their snouts to the ground. A rainbow of scales greets my gaze, all spread out over the enormous expanse of their Mountain, adding brilliance and life to this dark night.

"We are here to celebrate Tovra. His life was full. Friend, warrior, lover, father, brother. He will be missed, but he is joining our kin who have passed before. His scales will add vibrance to every rainbow. His fire will add brilliance to the stars. But his love stays behind with us."

I turn, dropping my head to nuzzle the top of Tovra's head. "Rest well, my friend." My voice drops to a whisper. "And thank you. Thank you for her."

Discreetly, I work a claw under one of his smaller scales, pulling it free and sliding it into the magic that holds my human form.

Lifting my head, I step back and nod to Tatha and Kogra. They stand, and every dragon follows their lead. Pride swells through me. My Mate is strong. She's kind. She's a leader. I will work every day, every hour, to be the male she deserves.

As one, we all lift our heads into the wind and thrashing snow, releasing a great roar. The Mountain shakes, and the deep rumble of an avalanche sounds below us. The snow flakes lift and dance in the sound-waves that echo for a long time across the vast range around us. When silence falls, Tatha and Kogra breathe a gentle stream of fire into the ground, turning in a tight circle. The rest of the clan joins in, moving and swaying their heads as they spin, each creating a charred mark of the Mountain clan—a circle with a v-shape in its center.

I direct my fire into the ground, turning my own circle, the top edge of my design aligning with Tovra's snout. My fire goes deeper, burns hotter, melting the hard rock until my royal symbol glows under my feet. As it cools, the large circle around me turns black—as black as my scales and shadows. In the very center there's a section of untouched stone left in the shape of a flame—my royal symbol.

I shift back onto my hind legs, standing tall, wings spread. White-hot fire erupts from my mouth, molten lava dripping from the corners of my lips.

I know my eyes are glowing white hot—I can see the brilliant reflection on the falling snow. Tatha's eyes widen as she takes in my power. Not every dragon can produce magma, and I've never known another who could maintain a flow like this. Dragon fire can penetrate dragon scales, but my magma melts dragon hide on contact. Kogra actually backs up a pace as my molten fire hits Tovra's body, and his scales spit and sizzle as they curl and lift away from his body.

Horn, claws, flesh, and bone melt. Just before it hardens, I vibrate the air in my lungs until my chest rumbles. Ash rises from Tovra's body as my molten fire mellows to flickering flames. The burning embers of Tovra's remains lift and dance among the falling snowflakes. The wind snatches them and carries Tovra into the sky to melt into the clouds to dance forever in the sky, where all dragons should spend their afterlife.

I feel a tug of sorrow and turn my head toward Tatha. Her amethyst eyes are soft and turned up, following the last traces of her father as they climb the wind currents. Her sadness presses against my heart, but there are no tears, and her back is straight. Kogra's face is wet with his tears, and without looking, Tatha's tail snakes out and rests against her brother's bright yellow hide.

A flare of unwanted jealousy rushes through my blood, but pride and compassion push the ugly feeling aside. Her pain is sharp, but she still comforts her brother.

She is a queen. My queen.

I cross to her, pressing my body into her side. Her tail slides away from her brother to curl around me, and I purr with love for her.

My heart stutters. For a moment, it feels as if the fire in my veins freezes as that realization hits me. *Love.*

The bond draws me to her. I want her every waking moment. It's a near compulsion to touch her. I live for her smile, her laugh, her temper. I crave the taste of her arousal on my tongue. Does all this add up to love? Because I do. I love her. Fiercely. I'll do anything for her.

Anything.

Her head presses to the side of my neck. The amethyst of her scales looks even more vibrant and beautiful against my black scales. I stretch my wing, resting it over her back.

We stand like that for a long time. The shuffle of claws along rock, and feet crunching through snow flows in my ears as the Mountain clan dragons retreat into their Mountain. Kogra is the last to turn away. His eyes travel over his sister, watching her upturned face that's wet with snow but free of tears. Worry pinches his eyes for a moment, but then he looks at me. I nod to him, and he bows, some of the concern melting from his face.

Silently, he walks off, and Tatha and I are alone on the beautiful plateau on the side of her Mountain. An hour passes, then another. The snow picks up, gathering around us. Our bodies glisten with melted snow, and still we remain. I will sit here with my Mate for days if that's what she needs.

Eventually, she sighs. Her voice is quiet but strong as she lifts her front leg, pointing toward the southern sky. "Hiding behind the clouds, right there, is the star my father named Galloris, after my mother. It's a small star, one you would easily miss among the many, but my father noticed her like he noticed that star. I'm told she was a steel-grey dragon who was easy to overlook with the brilliance of colors around her. But father saw her vibrance. He says I have the same spark."

I brush her head with my snout. "I didn't know her well, but I actually met her a few times before the clan moved here to the Mountain. She was kind. Quiet. Reserved. She must have been saving that spark for her true love. And she definitely passed it to you, Heilsi."

She rubs the top of her head against my chin, and I purr against her. We fall silent for a long while before she turns toward me but her gaze is lowered. "Do you think my brother will make a good clan leader?"

I consider her question for a moment. "I don't know him well. But these past few days have shown me a dragon of character. He cares. Even though he has been away from his clan, he has an easy rapport with the dragons who live here. I think your people would find it easy to follow him." I glance down at her, but she keeps her eyes on the sky. "Is that what you want, Tatha?"

She's silent for several minutes before shrugging. "I'm not sure. I love my clan. I love the Mountain. But without my father ..." Her breath stutters, but still, no tears fall. "I don't know if this will still feel like home without him."

"You don't have to decide now. Follow your heart. Stay if you need to."

Her face finally tilts up toward me, and I search her eyes for a hint of her thoughts, but she just stares at me. Her words come out in a whisper. "If I follow my heart, it will lead me to you." Her head drops, and her shoulders slump under my wing. "But Kem, does my heart only pull to you because of the bond? Biologically, I *need* to be near you. But ..."

I rest my head on hers, breathing in her spicy earthiness around the crisp, clean scent of snow. My heart squeezes, and my lungs feel like they are unable to fill with enough air as I say, "The bond is strong, but Mates have been rejected, Tatha. If your heart feels I am not the right fit for you, despite the call of the bond, you can turn me down. You can sever—"

"No!"

I press my lips together as she shoves her face into my chest. "Fuck. No, Kemremir. I may need some time to wrap my head around this bond and what my future might look like, but my heart knows." Her soft chuckle eases some of my tension.

I pull her tighter to my body. "There's no rush, Heilsi. I ... can be patient."

She laughs against my chest. "I can tell that was hard for you to say. But thank you, Kem." Silence stretches between us again until the soft blue blush of morning lightens the heavy clouds. "Are you heading back to the valley today?"

I try to hold back a growl at her words. *You* heading back, not *we*. I nod. "Yes. The sooner I take care of Inchel and his little insurrection, the sooner I can put all my focus on my Mate."

I purr against her, and arousal spears through me at her shiver. She smirks up at me, her sharp teeth bright against the pull of her lips. "And running the kingdom, of course."

"Yes, that too."

She chuckles, sliding out from under my wing. I'm never physically cold, but without her pressed to my side, I feel an emptiness that has a chill to it.

We walk single-file down the path and back into the Mountain. Kogra greets us at the entrance, bowing to me. "Your Majesty, thank you again for making an exception for my father. I know it meant a great deal to him to be Elevated here."

"Of course, Kogra. It was my honor." I glance at Tatha with

95

a smile. "After all, the North Lake is a tradition, not a law." Kogra nods, and I continue, "I need to go back to the valley."

Kogra frowns. "The Challenge."

I turn to Tatha. "See to your people."

I flick my gaze back to Kogra. "If you're serious about standing with me in support, pick a few of your trusted guards to come with us."

Stepping closer to Tatha, I breathe her in. For the first time in ... since the caves under the Unseelie castle ... I feel fear—real, sharp, knee-buckling, breath-stealing fear. Tatha leans back to look me in the eyes, and I brush my tail along her body. "If I lose"—She starts shaking her head, but I press on—"If I lose, Tatha, double your guards. Don't let Inchel bully you or your clan. You are fierce, Heilsi. Stand your ground. Be strong for your people. Don't—"

"I'm going with you, Kem." Her eyes sparkle with rage-tinged determination. "I will watch my Mate win. I will be there as you tear that slimy green dragon to pieces." Her wings flap in fury. "I will be with you."

Fuck, she's glorious.

"Heilsi, you are beyond words."

Kogra speaks, but I keep my eyes on Tatha. "Sister, go with your Mate in the knowledge I will watch over our clan. I know there is no possibility of Inchel getting through the King as well as my sister, but I will hold our Mountain if that impossibility happens."

Slowly, Tatha peels her eyes from mine, smiling at her brother. "Thank you."

I press a wing to her shoulder. "Are you sure, Tatha? You don't have to co—"

"I'm coming, *Mate*."

I nod with a smile, turning with her to face the narrow

path through the mountain range. "Then, there's no time like the present."

Kogra barks at the two guards flanking the cave entrance, "Go with them."

"No." Tatha turns to her brother. "You will need every dragon here ... in case." Kogra's eyes darken. "Besides, I'll be with him." She jerks her head at me, and I nod at Kogra, giving him a silent promise. "And the King has many guards and allies. I'll be fine, Kogra."

With a swish of her wings, she grins at me over her shoulder. "Shall we?"

She leaps off the ledge, and my wings carry me after her.

I can't lose. I won't lose.

Banking over Tatha, I look back at my Mate. Her purple scales flash in brilliant contrast against the stone and snow of the steep mountains around us.

There's too much on the line.

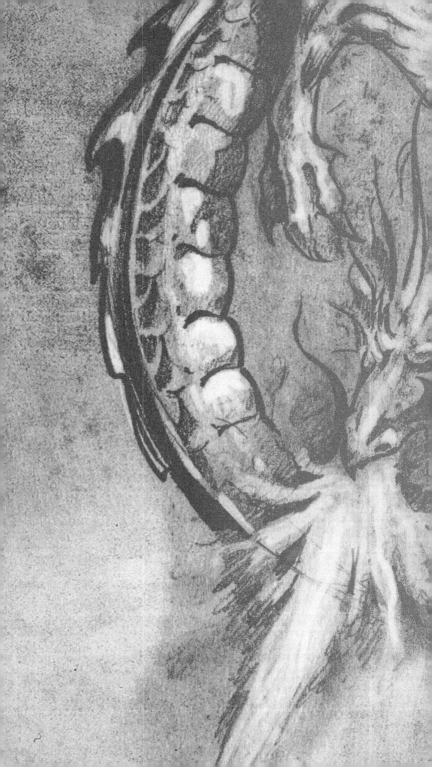

10

TATHA

EVEN THOUGH, just a few days ago I swore I wouldn't return to the valley, it didn't surprise me when I fought to return. In fact, saying those words released something in my chest that I wasn't aware I was holding.

But the Challenge is a constant worry in my mind, and with each beat of my wings, another rock drops in the pit of my stomach. By the time Kem and I touch down in the valley, landing right in the royal gardens, my chest is tight again and my back is in knots. I roll my neck as I shift, my body becoming smaller, the world growing larger. The solid stone steps anchor me as we climb toward the castle doors, but Kem pauses, pressing his large warm hand to my lower back. He leans down, and I'm surrounded by his scent and his shadows. His lips hover over mine, his breath fanning over my heated face. "I'm going to meet with Syphe and a few of my guards to catch up on what I've missed while away. I also need to be updated on Inchel."

My face tightens, and my lips pull back at the mention of the one Challenging my Mate. Kem's finger strokes down my cheek, and I shiver, forgetting my rage as desire floods my body. "You are welcome to come with me, Heilsi."

I shake my head, the movement small to keep from dislodging his hand from my face. "I will leave you to your duties."

My gaze jumps between his dark eyes and his tempting lips. It's on the tip of my tongue to ask why he never took me in our dragon forms, but the words die as Kem smiles.

"You *are* a distraction." He backs up, pulling me with him until he's pressed to the exterior wall of his castle. His face closes in, and his lips brush softly against mine. It's a gentle kiss, just a light touch of lips, but my entire body hums. "But a most welcome distraction, Tatha."

The days of teasing in the mountains finally break me, and before I realize I've moved, I rise to my toes, my hands grasping the back of his neck. I pull him to me in a fierce kiss, and our tongues slide together. His shadows curl around us until they completely block out the afternoon light. Kem's arm snakes around my waist, and his erection presses into my belly. I groan against his lips, and his chest rumbles with a low growl as he angles his head to take the kiss deeper.

Why didn't he take my dragon? Why only now—?

A foreign touch crawls under the hem of my dress. One of Kem's hands is threaded through my hair, the other is wrapped around my waist, so what ...?

I yank my head back. Looking around, it's like Kem and I are in a bubble of swirling mists, smoke, and shadow. Not a speck of light leaks through. And when I glance down, I gasp as tendrils of Kem's shadows curl up my legs, tickling my skin, moving slowly under my dress.

My eyes snap back to him, and a wicked smile lights up his face. My voice is breathy, as I pant, "Kem, what are—?"

"Just let me feel you, Mate. I've been trapped in a cave with your beautiful scent driving me mad for days."

"Then why didn't—"

My words choke off on a gasp as Kem's shadows slide under my panties and stroke between my folds. I'm so wet, and the cool tingling brush of his shadows against my pussy jerks my body harder against his. My head falls back, and Kem's grip in my hair tightens. His shadows flick against my clit and slide down my dress between my breasts to tease my nipples.

I moan and pant as I grind against his body. It's as if he's everywhere at once. His touch echoes through his shadows. I'm breathless as he brings every nerve ending to life. Even though I'm still dressed, every inch of skin vibrates with his caresses.

Kem's lips trail across my jaw and down my neck. "You are glorious, my Mate." His teeth nip at my pulse as his shadows slide inside me, curling and expanding. I bite my lip so hard, the coppery taste of blood coats my throat as I swallow. He whispers, "You are safe with me. No sound can leave the shield of my power."

His shadows stroke deep while flicking my clit and licking my breasts. My body is alive with pleasure, but I can't help but think what a passerby might think at seeing a swirling mass of shadows along the castle wall.

Kem tugs my hair, and I peel my eyes open to find him a breath from my face. Red fire rims his eyes, edging to blue, then pure white at the center. "Later, Mate, I will have my cock inside you as you ride me hard, but right now, Heilsi"—his tongue darts out, licking my lips—"I want to watch you come, right here, right now."

I buck against the pressure of his shadows, and as I'm held captive under Kem's stare, they curl and press in just the right spot. They stroke, expand, pump, curl, and thrust. I'm completely filled.

Kem's voice feathers over my ear, "Give me your orgasm. Come for me."

The throbbing between my thighs explodes, and the flood of bliss is almost a stinging pain as I come. It's the most glorious pain, snapping around the pleasure. I'm lost in the euphoria. My mouth opens on a silent scream, and Kem's eyes turn pure white, like burning phosphorus as he watches me come undone. His shadows continue to lick and stroke me, carrying me through my orgasm and straight into another.

I can't breathe. The shadows are relentless with a tickling sensation that is somehow both warm and cool. My knees buckle as pulse after pulse of pleasure rocks through me, but Kem easily holds me up with hands, his power, and his shadows.

Slowly, I come back to my senses, gasping to catch my breath. I get my feet back under me, realizing I have partially shifted, and I've sunk my claws into the flesh of Kem's biceps. Carefully, I extract myself, and Kem hisses, but it's not pain on his face, it's deep, wild desire.

All I can do is gaze into his face as his hands curl around my jaw, holding me still. "You are magnificent, Tatha."

My face flushes with heat, and his smile grows. His fingers comb through my tangled hair and his shadows smooth down my dress. My wet panties are uncomfortable, and I shift slightly, wishing I could just take them off.

Kem's shadows pull away from me, slowly melting into his

skin. I duck my head, noticing the hard length of his cock straining against his pants. "What about you?"

His large hand brushes down my hair again, landing on my shoulder, and I sink into his warmth. "I can wait a bit longer, Heilsi. I needed your release. Mine will come later. Anticipation, remember?" The shadows are gone, and I'm relieved to see we are alone on the steps. "I enjoy the build-up."

My core flutters, and my damp panties get wetter at his words.

He brushes a light kiss over my lips, mimicking the kiss that started all this, then steps back. "Anything you need, all you have to do is ask. Anyone in the castle will help you. I will find you later." And with one last quick kiss, Kem turns and strides through the castle doors.

I turn a tight circle, feeling silly, and turned on, and a bit lost. What now? I didn't want to crowd Kem, but what should I do now?

"Can I help you with anything, my Lady?"

I nearly jump out of my skin, turning to face a beautiful woman with liquid silver hair. She's wearing the royal armor, and my blush deepens as I pull at the hem of my dress, certain it's wrinkled in an obvious way. But the woman's face is impassive as she waits for my response.

I sigh, a soft laugh spilling from my lips. "I guess I'm not sure."

The corner of her lips lift slightly, and a mischievous look passes over her eyes. "I was headed to the training room. Would you like to come?"

My brows lift with interest. "Yes! That would be great, thank you."

She nods with a smile. "Arvun."

"Nice to meet you, Arvun. I'm Tatha."

"Yes, I know. Nice to meet you."

And ... my blush is back.

Arvun sweeps her arm toward the castle doors, and I step forward. She falls into step beside me. "I'm sorry about your father."

A pang of sadness claws at my chest, but it's not as sharp as it was yesterday. "Thank you. He was ready. He was at peace."

"That is good. It is a sad occasion, but I always find the Elevation ceremony deeply beautiful."

"As do I."

We travel slowly through the castle, Arvun occasionally pointing out areas and rooms, giving me a tour along the way. It is small compared to my Mountain home, but Kem's castle is much larger than I first thought. The soaring ceilings and nearly endless glass windows and doors give the building an airy open feel that my cave can't match.

As we turn a corner, a curving staircase leads downward, but Arvun slows. A smile lifts her face, and her pale skin pinks at her cheeks. I follow her gaze, landing on a woman walking our way.

I thought Arvun was beautiful, but this woman is beyond that. She's stunning. She's luminescent. A thick braid of emerald green hair crowns her head, trailing down her back, leaving her delicate face on display. Her eyes shine like gemstones, and her smile is the kind of smile that could devastate kingdoms.

And that smile is aimed at Arvun.

The emerald woman draws to a stop before us. "Arvun. I was looking for you, but here I find you with another woman" —her eyes travel over my body, but there's laughter in her voice—"and quite a beauty at that."

I hold up a hand, ready to set the record straight, but

Arvun laughs. "Knock it off, Ziza. This is Tatha." Arvun turns to me. "Tatha, may I introduce Ziza, my wife."

I try to keep my face neutral, but I feel my eyes going wide. Ziza chuckles, shrugging a shoulder. "Ah, I see the King told you the story. Yes, I'm *that* Ziza." The smile slides from her face. "I'm lucky to be alive, and I have Raelyn to thank for my life."

Arvun steps forward, tucking her finger under Ziza's chin, lifting her gaze. "It's in the past. You have to let it go."

A sad smile spreads across Ziza's face. "I'm trying. It was a big blunder."

My fists clench as Arvun caresses Ziza's face.

Our second day in the Mountain, Kem did tell me about Ziza. This emerald dragon is the one who Challenged Raelyn, the Seelie queen. She did so in an act of rebellion against Kem, and I can't help the flutter of anger that tightens my chest.

Ziza shrugs off Arvun's touch, her eyes finding mine. "I *am* sorry."

I don't know why she's apologizing to me, but Arvun grips her shoulders, pulling Ziza's attention back to her. "The King knows you're sorry. He has forgiven you. Raelyn has forgiven you." She presses a kiss to Ziza's lips. "Time to forgive yourself."

A sliver of my anger drains away at Arvun's loving words. There was no resentment or lingering anger in Kem's voice when he told me the story. He has forgiven Ziza.

Ziza sighs, stepping back from Arvun. "I'm working on it. But we don't need to burden Tatha with my moods." She glances over her shoulder toward the stairs. "You headed to the training room?" Arvun nods. "Then I will leave you to it." She turns to me, bowing slightly. "Have fun, my Lady." Ziza smirks at Arvun. "I have a feeling the one fated for Kemremir will have an unexpected fierceness, so good luck."

Arvun glances at me. "Indeed."

I smile at the women, holding my hands out at my sides. "I have been known to 'throw down,' but I've never fought in this form."

Arvun places a hand on my shoulder, nudging me toward the stairs. "Then let's go see what you've got."

Ziza turns, calling over her shoulder. "See you at dinner. Tatha, if the King's business takes his time into the evening, feel free to join us." She turns the corner before I can respond, but I have a feeling, no matter what, Kem will find time for me tonight.

Arvun chuckles, the sound keeping time with our descending steps. "I don't think you have to worry about being left to your own devices tonight." I almost stumble, my small human feet scrambling to catch on the next step as Arvun continues, "Being newly mated is intense, or so I've been told. He won't be able to stay away."

I duck my head, trailing my hand along the cool stone wall. Am I losing my identity? Will I forever be known as the King's mate? Is that all I am now?

My spiraling thoughts and the winding stairs begin to make me dizzy, but we finally reach the bottom, and my mouth falls open as I cross the room.

'Room' is too simple a word. A giant space spills out before me. Columns of white and gold marble hold up the ceiling that stretches so far overhead, shadows obscure just how high this room soars. The stone floor spreads before us, occasionally dotted with worn carpets in what looks like different sparring areas. An apricot haired man moves through a warmup stretch far off to the left. A pair of people spar on a carpet further into the room. Their claw-tipped hands swipe with deadly precision, their colorful hair a blur with their movements. A rack of weapons glimmers to my right, and a sky-blue-haired woman sits on a low cushion, cleaning a row of blades. It's strange to see weapons here. Dragons consider ourselves the weapon in battle, even in human form. My father raised me to believe forged weapons were beneath us. The woman's eyes flick to us briefly before dropping back to her task.

Arvun must notice my lingering expression. "Some of us like to train with weapons, especially those of us who routinely go off world. We may not use them often, but it helps to be versed in how each feels and moves. Knowledge always gives you an edge."

I nod. That makes sense.

Further down the wall, there's an open chest containing wraps and gloves, along with salves and cleaning agents.

Despite the others in this room, the space is quiet, the clanking of steel, and the thud of punches seem muted as they get lost in the towering height of the room.

I'm pulled from my wandering observations by Arvun's voice. "So, where do you want to start?"

I smile, excitement building. "What were you planning to do today?"

"I was going to work on blade drills, but since you're here, wanna spar?"

"Hand to hand?"

Arvun shrugs out of her armor, the leather and metal thudding against the floor. "Oh, I knew I'd like you."

I match her grin as we head toward a large rug. It's worn, the pattern nearly gone in places where countless feet have shuffled over its surface. But it's surprisingly soft under my boots, cushioning my steps from the hard stone.

I kick my boots off, flinging them to the side, and Arvun

does the same. Crossing my left foot before my right, I pace in a slow circle around the edge of the rug, and Arvun mirrors me. I flex my toes, feeling strength carry up my calves, into my thighs, and stabilizing my core. My dragon strength is here, I just have to learn how to use it within my human form.

Arvun is giving me time. She's watching me. She's learning me ... how I move, what my weaknesses are.

I prefer to learn by doing, so I dig my left foot into the rug, catching traction in the rough weave, and launch at Arvun. She smiles as she charges to meet me, and I smile in answer.

Our fists fly, rarely making contact at first. We each swing a few kicks, dodging and ducking. Before long, sweat beads my skin, sticking my thigh-length dress to me. With every pivot, every punch, every kick ... I get more comfortable with my body, and Arvun loses her playfulness as she realizes she now has to concentrate against my attacks.

Power flows from my core as I land a punch to her ribs. I spin to avoid her roundhouse kick, but she clips me on the shoulder.

Around and around we dance. I lose track of how long we spar, measuring time in punches landed, in bruises forming from Arvun's landed blows. Sweat drips from my skin, soaking into the rug, and Arvun's silver hair has darkened to a metal gray with the sweat that plasters her short hair to her head.

With my next attack, I feint right, push left, and spring off the floor. My momentum carries me up her body, and I wrap my leg around her neck, throwing my body to the side and down. We spin, and I bring her to the mat, following my momentum to land kneeling on her chest. Her eyes are wide, but she smiles as she slams an arm between my thighs and flips me on my back. I land with a thud, but instead of following through with a punch to my gut like I would have done, she rolls away and jumps to her feet.

I do the same, and as we circle each other again, a slow clap pauses our movement.

I know it's him before I turn, and when I do, there's Kem, his skin blending with the natural shadows of the room as he stalks toward us. Wiping a hand down my face, my breath hitches for a whole new reason as I watch his muscled body approach.

Arvun bows. "Your Majesty."

"Ziza figured you lost track of time down here. I told her I'd send you on your way when I came to fetch my Mate." I swallow, managing to peel my eyes from Kem, looking around the large space. It's empty, and the lack of windows steals any indication of the time of day. "The dinner hour has come and gone. Come, Tatha. Let's let Arvun get to her wife."

"Oh! I'm so sorry, Arvun. I didn't realize it was so late. Please, extend my apologies to Ziza."

Arvun laughs, hooking her armor over her shoulder. "I would have stopped our session had I wanted to. Ziza can afford to practice patience. I was having fun."

I smile. "Me too. Thank you."

Arvun moves toward the staircase. "My pleasure. I'd love to spar with you again, Tatha. Anytime."

"I'd like that as well."

I hadn't heard him move, but Kem's breath flutters over my cheek as he leans over me from behind, whispering in my ear. "You were dazzling. I'd like to spar with you as well, Heilsi."

Turning, my chest brushes against his body, and my eyes travel up to meet his hungry face. "I'd like that."

He nods, holding my gaze a moment before taking my hand and leading me from the room and up the stairs.

I assume he's taking us back to his rooms, but after a few moments, I realize we are going in the opposite direction. Kem must notice my swiveling gaze because he squeezes my hand.

"We're headed to the dining hall. I figured you'd be hungry. But first, there's someone I want you to meet."

He leads me down two halls and up a short staircase. At the top, he turns to a simple wood door, opening it on silent hinges. I stall in the doorway, gasping. A short forest-green-haired woman sitting at a table littered with books and scrolls lifts her head with a smile, bowing to Kem. "Ah, your Majesty. This is her, I presume?"

Kem pulls me into the room, releasing my hand. "Yes, this is Tatha, my Mate. Tatha, this is Sabina, the royal scribe."

My eyes travel the room with greedy attention. The room is well lit with flickering flames encased in glass. I tilt my head back, marveling at the books and scrolls stacked along every wall from the floor to the very high ceiling. My mouth is open in awe as I turn back to Sabina. "It's an honor to meet you. You have the *best* job!"

Kem chuckles, and Sabine's smile is bright. "I think so, yes. The King mentioned you might have some books you'd like copied?"

In my panic, every book I've ever coveted leaves my brain. Sabine laughs. "It's okay. Just send a list when you've compiled one."

I nod, my gaze wandering around the room again. Oh, the stories on these shelves.

Warmth presses into my back, and Kem's fingers flex as he nudges me toward the door. "Let's get you fed, Mate. Later, we can work on your list of books."

I can't help but look over my shoulder as we enter the hall, and Kem practically has to pull me away from the scribe's room. "That is ... spectacular. Your own scribe. Right here."

"And of course, there's the library. The largest in the Realm. You're welcome to borrow any book you want. A perk of being human. No need to wait for a copy."

That's true. Books and sex are two huge tics in the human column. My lips pull up in a teasing smile as Kem strides through a tall set of open doors. Still holding my hand, Kem leads me into the vast dining hall. Long wooden tables stretch the length of the room. A couple dozen people sit scattered among the tables in a mix of chairs and benches. The rumble of voices grinds to a halt as Kem crosses the room, me in tow. Every head bows before going back to their meals and conversations.

Kem pulls out a chair for me at a table with three others seated down its length. I sink into the wood seat, all too aware of my sweaty dress, and probably messy hair. But nobody seems to take notice; they simply bow to me before going back to their meals.

I tilt my head back to look up his towering body as Kem's palm caresses my shoulder, sliding down my arm.

"I'll go get us food. I'll be right back."

My brows pinch. Wouldn't the King be served his food? Why is he getting his own plate?

A man sitting across from me chuckles, and I whip my head toward him. He pulls a piece of meat off his fork with his teeth, talking around the mouthful of food. "Kemremir likes to do things for himself. We tried for years to serve him, but eventually we gave up. He's as stubborn as he is strong."

I glance over my shoulder, catching Kem laughing with a crimson-haired man who scoops some kind of sauce onto both plates Kem holds in his hands. Turning back to the man before me, I smile. "I like that."

The man sitting two seats down on my left chuckles. "Aye. We do as well, now that we're used to it."

I smile at him, and he bows. "I'm Bran."

Ah, so this sky-blue man belongs to Syphe. His leather cuff looks worn and loved. His doesn't have the copper banding that Syphe's does. Instead, delicate copper and blue threads create a pattern of two dancing dragons—him and Syphe. My throat burns with the urge to cry at the beauty of their bond.

As if thinking her name summoned her, Syphe crosses the hall, throwing her leg over the bench where her mate sits, pressing a kiss to his lips before he slides a plate before her. "My love."

She grabs her fork, spearing a roasted vegetable and bringing it between her lips. "You are too good to me."

Bran presses another kiss to her lips, licking the oil and spice from her mouth. "And don't you forget it."

She hums. "Never."

The man across the table chuckles. "Okay you two, take it to your rooms if you can't keep it in your pants." Syphe flings a roll at him, and he catches it one handed, biting into it, releasing the sweet and sour aroma into the air. He looks at me with a smile, his pale yellow hair falling over his eyes. "I'm Undreth, another of the King's guards along with Syphe and Hiti here." He stabs a thumb toward the cerulean-haired woman sitting a few places down to his right. She nods at me, but remains silent as she focuses back on her meal.

A plate slides before me, and Kem sits to my right. "Undreth, you already causing trouble?"

"No."

Syphe and Bran bark twin laughs. "Yes."

"Hey! I was not!"

Syphe chucks a roasted carrot at Undreth, and he dodges it while throwing his knife at her. I gasp, but she catches it by the hilt, spinning it in her hand before stabbing the large slab of meat on her plate. "Thanks."

Everyone chuckles, and I find myself laughing along.

These people have easily welcomed me into their group ... but as Kemremir's Mate. A tiny kick of uncertainty sours my stomach. I am a leader among my people. The Mountain clan has always looked to me as my father's successor. But here, I'm just ... his.

The table quiets as everyone resumes their meals, and I push my food around my plate. Kem leans toward me, his heat brushing against my side. "What's troubling you? Heilsi?"

Attention around the table shifts to me, and I fight to keep from squirming in my seat. I know I need to talk to him about this, but it doesn't seem like the right place. Kem brushes my tangled hair over my shoulder. "For someone who just spent hours in the training room, you're much too tense."

Undreth spears a nearly raw piece of meat on his plate before shoving it in his mouth. "Hours?"

I shrug, but Kem sits back, draping his arm behind my chair. "You should have seen her. She took Arvun to the mat."

Undreth stops chewing, and Syphe does a slow clap that reddens my cheeks. "Well done. I call next when you want to spar again."

Undreth raises his fork. "Then the nickname makes sense, fierce one. Put me on your sparring dance card."

Kem pats the back of my chair, the gentle vibration traveling down my spine before he turns back to his plate, and everyone tucks back into their dinners. I glance at my Mate from the corner of my eye. Did he suspect the reason behind my unease? Can he read me so easily already?

Light conversation drifts around the table, and Hiti, who has been mostly silent, raises her glass to me before turning back to her almost empty plate. Kem notices, shifting so his thigh brushes against mine. "They like you, Heilsi. Warriors recognizing kindred spirits."

Just like that, the sour churning in my stomach eases. I've always been an overthinker; stuck in my spiraling thoughts. And that bad habit has kept me from seeing how genuine these people are treating me. Maybe I'm the only one who's putting me in the box of 'only Kem's Mate.'

Silently, I vow to do my best to view myself with truth, and not through my insecurities.

Grabbing my fork, I pick through the variety of meats, vegetables, and a lump of something gelatinous. Kem chuckles, low enough that I'm the only one who hears it as he leans back over. "Just try a little of everything. See what you like."

His deep voice hints at a double meaning, and I press my thighs together. What I'd like is for him to take me back to his room and deliver on his earlier promise. His nostrils flare, and his chest rumbles with a little chuckle. "Eat first, Heilsi."

I swallow, realizing he scented my arousal, and around the smell of meat and spice and oil, I catch his arousal as well.

I focus on my plate, trying a small piece of potato first, finding its texture pleasant, and the flavors of fat and salt quite delicious. After that first taste, I tuck into my meal, enjoying every bite.

Pushing my clean plate away, I sit back, drink in hand, content.

But my dinner sours in my stomach at Hiti's quiet words from down the table. "We will have extra guards on your doors tonight, Kemremir. Just in case Inchel tries anything."

Kem shakes his head, but Syphe chimes in. "The Challenge is tomorrow, and we're not taking any chances."

Tomorrow! No. I'm not ready.

But Kem smiles, finishing the last of his meal. "Fine. I'll just be glad when all this is behind us." His fork hits his plate with a quiet clink as he turns to face me. "I have other things I'd like to focus on."

I have trouble getting my lungs to fill, but everyone at the table raises their glasses. "Here, here!"

I should be embarrassed, but all I feel is pride. These

114

people love their King, and he loves them. My Mate is a good man, and I'm proud to be his.

There's a loud scrape of wood against stone as Kem pushes back from the table, grabbing my hand, hauling me to my feet. "Speaking of which. Please excuse us."

Bran and Syphe stand as well. "Us too."

Undreth sighs, running his hand through his tawny hair. "Ah, to be Mated."

Bran hugs Syphe to his side. "Don't give up hope, my friend. Your Mate is out there."

A frown pulls at my lips as Kem leads me away from the table. Yes, everyone has a Mate out there, but the chances of finding the one tied to your soul are so slim. It seems unfair that fate would hide your soulmate in the vastness of the universe like a needle in a haystack.

I'm so lost in my thoughts, I don't realize we've crossed the threshold to Kem's rooms. I catch the flash of three guards in the hall—Hiti, and two guards I haven't met yet—as the door clicks shut behind us. My melancholy fades away as Kem leads me to the washroom, turning on the shower. Before long, the large room starts to fill with steam, and the musical sound of the water hitting the crystal shower walls draws me in.

I peel my dirty dress over my head and step in the shower, sighing as I turn to let the water run down my back and over my head. My skin pebbles, even in the heat of the shower, as Kem's hand slides across my stomach and around my waist before pressing against my lower back.

His large body leans into mine, his hard cock pressing into my stomach. He growls, his chest vibrating against me. "Now, Heilsi. Now I will find my release inside your tight, hot cunt."

11

KEMREMIR

TWICE, I watched Tatha come apart in the shower, my cock aching to be inside her, but I held back—until now.

My Mate is spread out on the bed beneath me. Her back arches into my touch as my fingers and shadows trail down her neck, between her breasts, and over her trembling stomach. My cock twitches as a breathy gasp leaves her lips, and her hips buck into my touch as my fingers brush against her clit.

"Again." I grit my teeth, issuing the command, lightly stroking her over and over, and she obeys, bucking against my hand. My shadows caress her as her spine curves off the bed, pressing her peaked nipples toward me.

Fuck. I need her.

My hands trace a path down her legs, and I watch in fascination as her skin pebbles in the wake of my touch. On my knees between her thighs, chest lifted, I grab her ankles, hooking them over my shoulders as my shadows dive into her wet heat. My shadows vibrate in time with her squeezing muscles. She moans, and as my shadows fuck her, the sensation of her clenching, pulsing core echoes in my very soul.

She has consumed me. All I am is desire. My entire purpose in this moment is to bring her pleasure and to find pleasure in her.

"Fuck, Kem. It feels so good, but I need you."

She tries to lift her hips, reaching for my cock, but I press a hand to her lower belly, holding her in place.

"Yes, Heilsi." I hold her gaze as I grip my length and line up at her entrance. My shadows remain inside her, but they flex and move, giving me room to slide into her, making it an even tighter fit.

Tatha's eyes slide closed, and her head rolls back, exposing her neck to me. "Oh! Ooh! So full, Kem. It's too much."

Her sweet panting breaths coax me on, and I push in a little more. "So beautiful, how you take me, Tatha. You're doing so well, Mate."

Her heels press into my shoulders as I go deeper, and the sight of my cock sliding into her wet pussy nearly brings me to orgasm. My muscles bunch across my upper back, and midnight scales spread across my skin as I fight to keep from coming.

I bottom out, and my dragon roars inside me as her walls squeeze my length and shadows. My magic pushes at my skin, the usual tingling brush of the shift an almost painful sting. I grit my teeth, holding my dragon at bay. My hips jerk back, then slam forward as Tatha grips my forearms. Her blunt human nails have shifted to her sharp amethyst claws, and they sink into my skin and scales. My hand skims up from her stomach, pressing between her breasts. Sweat glistens along her skin, and my dragon growls, sending the vibration through my entire body and down my cock, and my shadows take that vibration and intensify it.

Tatha screams, trying to arch against the pleasure, but I hold her down. My hips pump into her as my shadows spread and curl inside her. A breeze wafts over my skin, and my next thrust slams even harder into her. I realize my wings have burst from my back, flapping with my driving hips. The tips of my wings brush the side walls of my large room, and I keep pumping into my Mate as my wings drive me on.

Falling forward, I wrap my arms around Tatha, and she clings to me, her hips lifting into my punishing rhythm. My wings lift us off the bed, and all I can think about is taking her as our dragons.

Later. Soon.

"I'm right there, Kem. Please. Oh! Yes! Come with me. Come with me, Mate!".

"Yes, Heilsi. I'm going to fill you with my cum until you're dripping with it."

My balls draw tight, and the building pressure in my lower back sparks to my core and up my spine. I throw my head back, roaring to the ceiling as Tatha comes again and I release into her.

It feels like my orgasm goes on and on as she pulses around me, and my shadows lick at her clit. My wings wrap around her, and we fall the short distance to the bed. I spin at the last second, landing on my back, bracing my Mate against my chest.

My wings slowly unfurl, but I hold tight to Tatha as we both struggle to slow our breathing.

The normal gentle wash of magic draws my wings into my

back and melts the scales from my skin. Tatha's talons change back to her delicate purple nails, and she rests her cheek on my chest with a sigh. "That was ..."

Her hair is damp with sweat, but still soft under my touch as I brush it back from her face. "Sublime, Mate. It was sublime."

"Yeah."

She burrows deeper into my chest, her arms hugging me tight. Crooking a finger under her chin, I try to lift her face, but she shakes her head, resisting my pull.

"What's wrong, Tatha?"

Her back expands with a great inhale, and her fingers dig into my skin with her exhale. "The Challenge."

Ah. My hands rub small circles on her back, and I kiss the top of her head. Taking a deep breath, our mingled scents float down my nose, settling in my soul. "Heilsi, I have fought and won over thirty Challenges, and Inchel is nowhere near the strength of some of my past opponents. I appreciate the concern, but please, try not to worry."

She nods, but I feel the tension in her back. "I just found you."

"And that"—I press another kiss to the top of her head— "is why you shouldn't worry. I have always fought for the kingdom, for the people, but now ... now I have you."

This time she allows me to lift her chin. Her bright amethyst eyes swim with tears, but they don't fall. As I apply more pressure under her chin, she crawls up my body, pressing her lips to mine. My heart stutters, and the heavy space in the center of my chest expands, filling with her.

"There's nothing and no one, Tatha, that has the power to keep me from you. You don't have to decide now, but know, if you want to continue to live in the Mountain, then that is where I'll be." She pulls back slightly, staring at my face. "It will take some work, but I can rule from anywhere. I can come down to the valley for council meetings and other such matters, and—"

"Kem." Her eyes dance back and forth between mine, her teeth biting her bottom lip before she continues, "Now that my father is gone, the Mountain won't be the same. I'm ... afraid to go back. He won't be there, and it hurts. It's silly because I knew this day was coming, and I thought I'd be prepared, but ..." Her head tilts down, her hair falling around her face as she stares at my chest. "If the clan agrees to appoint my brother as the new leader, maybe I'd like to try, you know, living here?"

I smile as I brush a hand down her hair then rub her back. "You don't sound so sure."

Her teeth worry at her lower lip again, and I'm tempted to kiss that swollen mouth. But my smile fades as she rolls off me. Propping myself on an elbow, I frown as she paces back and forth several times. Her fingers comb through her vibrant purple waves. Her gaze darts from the floor, to the walls, to the windows, back to the floor ... everywhere but me.

I wait her out, feeling her unease and frustration through our building bond.

Finally, she pauses her pacing, looking at me. "I just ... it's that ..." I remain silent through her long pause until finally she huffs, planting her hands on her hips. "At the Mountain, why didn't you claim me?"

I'm so taken aback, I can't get out a single word before she barrels on. "Because, Kemremir, I'm a dragon. *We* are dragons. No matter the bond between us, no matter what *Fate* has to say about us, I need someone who wants my dragon." She turns, pacing again, and I slowly stand, opening my mouth to correct her, but she talks over me. "Don't get me wrong, I love being with you in this form. It's ... beyond what I thought it could be, but Kemremir—"

Her squeak of surprise cuts off her words as my shadows snap away from me, engulfing the room in darkness, wrapping their tendrils around her body. They yank her to me, and I catch her, tightening my arms to the point I'm afraid I'm bruising her. She wraps her legs around my waist, and I hug her. The thought that she believed for one second I didn't want her dragon nearly tears my heart from my chest.

"Oh, Heilsi. I'm so sorry. You were grieving, and my dragon ... well, you've seen him. He's ... *more* than other dragons. I was ... afraid."

"Afraid? That I wouldn't want your dragon?"

I shake my head. "No. I was afraid I'd hurt you."

With a quick jerk of movement, she pushes her palms into my shoulders. Her eyes are narrow, spearing into me, and she pokes a finger into my chest. "I've been in my dragon form all my life. I do *love* sex with you in this form." A smirk crawls across my face as I run my hands down her back and squeeze her ass. She chuckles, but grinds into me with the movement. "But my dragon craves you. She ... needs you." Her nails grow and lengthen once again, and she drags them down my chest, a thin line of blood trailing the marks. I grow hard, and my hands tighten on her ass as her whispered words float through my shadows. "I can't really complain, since you were only being kind"—she kisses my cheek—"and considerate"—her lips press to my other cheek —"and caring"—she kisses my mouth and fire boils through my veins. When she pulls back slightly, her teasing smile nearly drives me to my knees. "But my dragon needs you, Mate."

A knock at the door out in the receiving room of my chambers stalls my response, and we both groan as her talons shrink down. I let her slide down my body until her feet hit the floor.

I turn and pause. Soft, pale light spills through the windows. Morning already? Where did the night go?

Tatha moves behind me, trailing a hand across my back, lighting up every nerve ending in my body. "I'm going to grab *another* shower."

I nod with a smile, crossing the room into my large walk-in wardrobe. Thoughts tumble through my mind as I dress quickly, imagining my dragon claiming hers, my claws sinking into her amethyst scales and riding her through our ecstasy.

As I leave the wardrobe, the soft sound of running water comes from the bathing room, and it takes all my strength to walk in the opposite direction toward the sitting room in the receiving area. A second knock sounds just as I close the bedroom door behind me.

"Enter."

Fynola enters, her lilac hair pulled back into a tight tail. Her strong arms flex slightly as she balances a large silver tray in her hands. "Breakfast, your Majesty?"

I nod over my shoulder to the table by the window. "None for me, but I'm sure Tatha is hungry."

Fynola crosses the room, setting the tray down with a gentle clink. Turning, her thumb and forefinger rub together, and I don't know that I've ever seen her make that nervous gesture before.

"What is it, Fynola?"

"Um, your Majesty, Kudrer requests your presence in the council chambers."

I almost snarl at the mention of the indigo dragon. He has always been one to side with Inchel, and I'm really not in the mood to hear whatever it is he has to say to me today.

But I nod. "Fine."

Fynola bows. "Anything else, your Majesty?"

"No, you're excused."

She hurries from the room, and I catch sight of the three guards in the hall before the door clicks shut behind her.

"Who was that?"

I turn, tension leaving my body as Tatha crosses the room. A towel is wrapped around her hair, and one of my shirts hangs down to her thighs. Her bare feet pad softly across the thick rug in the center of the room, and she props a hip on the edge of the table as she pops a piece of melon in her mouth.

Oh, to be that piece of fruit right now.

"Fynola. I'm needed in the council chambers."

A flicker of fear crosses her eyes, but she banishes it immediately with a bright smile, crossing to me and raising onto her toes. I lean down to meet her halfway, pressing a kiss to her warm lips.

She says, "Do what needs to be done. The world goes on, even with the Challenge looming, and I know you have duties. I'll find my way today. I'll keep busy. Then"—she kisses me again, tugging my bottom lip between her teeth, sucking softly—"I'll watch my Mate tear his opponent to pieces."

A low groan rumbles from my throat. "Yes, Heilsi." I cup her face. "Then you and I will celebrate as only dragons can."

Her pupils dilate, and a spark of her dragon fire lights in the centers of her eyes. I smile down at her, pressing another quick kiss to her lips before stepping away.

"I'll see you soon, Mate."

My long legs carry me down the hall, but I keep my pace slow. The guard has changed outside my rooms, and Arvun and Undreth follow me. A third guard stays at the doors to my chambers.

I take my time, stopping to talk to staff I pass along the

way, checking on the kitchens, making sure the cooks have everything they need for the upcoming Moneria celebration.

Let Kudrer wait.

I spend an hour walking through my castle before finally sighing, turning to my guards. "I guess I should see what Kudrer wants."

Undreth nods, but Arvun chuckles, her eyes dancing with amusement. "Aye, your Majesty. Kudrer has quite the temper. He might be storming through the castle as we speak, looking for you."

I match her smile, though it doesn't reach my eyes. There's so much I'd rather do than meet with the volatile indigo dragon.

But I am King. I have a duty.

Finally, approaching the council chamber doors, one is ajar, and I push it open, leaving my guards to stand post. The door remains open as I enter the room, my shadows peeling away from me in a show of power as my gaze lands on Kudrer.

"Ah, your Majesty. I'm sorry to pull you away from your Mate." I fight back a scowl, keeping my face blank. "Congratulations."

I nod, crossing my arms. "I hope this is not why you summoned me. You could have congratulated me at the Moneria celebration."

A smirk of a smile curls up his lips. "Oh, no, your Majesty."

When he doesn't continue, I let loose the growl I'd been holding back. "So?"

He paces a slow circle around the room, his shoes clicking loudly on the marble floor as he passes over each of the embedded emblems representing the clans.

"A member of my clan submitted a visitor application this last round, and was denied."

Another long pause has my temper rising, but I hold my

ground. Keeping my face blank, I let my shadows expand, reaching for the light spilling through the towering windows.

Kudrer swallows. "I would like to know why, on behalf of my clan member."

Really? He knows the rules.

A sliver of tension curls up my spine, but I take a deep breath. The sooner I deal with Kudrer, the sooner I can move on with my day.

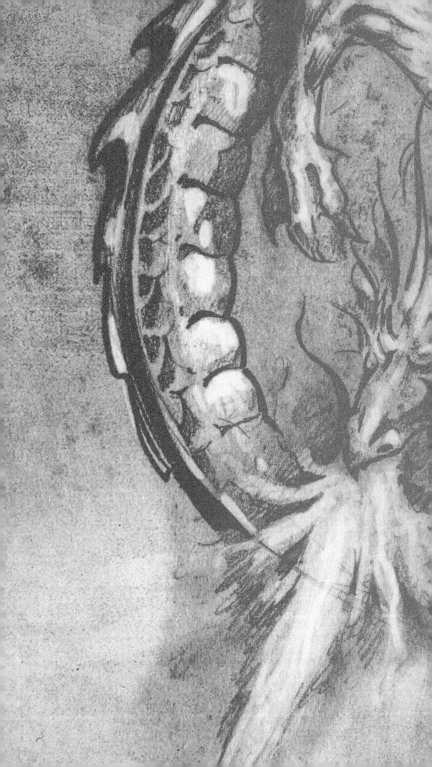

12

TATHA

AFTER FINISHING MY BREAKFAST, missing Kem the entire time, I enter the wardrobe, tossing my wet towel into the bathroom on the way. Finger-combing my hair, I pick out a soft pair of stretchy gray pants and a form-fitting sleeveless top in black. I take the time to write down several books I'd love to have copied, doing my best to keep the list short. Tucking it in my back pocket, I slide into my boots and head out of Kem's rooms.

There's a new guard at the doors, and he follows me as I stroll down the halls. The castle grows brighter as the sun climbs the sky, refracting light through the crystal walls. Rainbows dance across my skin, and I lift my hand as I walk, dancing my fingers through the beams of light.

It really is beautiful here.

A man with metal-gray hair passes with an armful of papers and books. He bows quickly before hurrying past.

Turning the next corner, I almost slam into a woman with burnt-orange hair, and she fumbles to her right to avoid colliding with me. To keep from falling, I press a hand to the wall, the cool crystal grounding me. Frustration clenches my teeth at still having these moments of clumsiness in this form. But the woman simply smiles. "So sorry, my Lady. Please excuse me."

She hurries past, and the guard at my back presses his hand to my shoulder. My muscles stiffen at the contact, but he doesn't seem to notice as his fingers squeeze slightly. "Are you alright, my Lady?"

Stepping away from the wall and out from under his hand, I nod, continuing on. "I'm fine. Thank you."

My stride slows, then stops as I pass a pair of open doors. The library. Shelves line the room, every space filled with books. Large wood tables divide the room down the center, and cozy overstuffed chairs occupy light-filled nooks. Sunlight spills into the room from the large windows, and through a pair of glass doors, a covered balcony leads toward a part of the castle gardens I haven't seen before.

Stepping into the room, my footsteps go silent as I sink into a plush rug that spreads from bookshelf to bookshelf. A short man with violet hair, some grey threading through his trimmed beard, pauses with his arm raised, a book in his hand halfway pushed into its place on the shelf. He bows his head before shelving the book and grabbing a stack of books from a nearby table, shuffling down a row of shelves.

Movement catches my eye from a far corner, and a man with ochre hair bows to me as he crosses his legs, sinking deeper into a large chair, a book propped in his lap.

The guard comes up to my side, standing too close. His fire-red hair flashes in my peripheral. "Is there anything in particular you'd like me to help you find, my Lady?"

I look around, biting my lip. How I'd love to spend the entire day exploring this library. But I don't think I could enjoy myself with this guard breathing down my neck, so I shake my head. Reaching into my pocket, I pull out the list. "I do have this I'd like to get to Sabine."

He takes the paper, lifting his head as he turns, shouting, "Dindris!"

I wince at his tone. Didn't anyone ever tell him not to yell in a library?

The violet-haired man speed-walks around a line of shelves. "Yes, sir?"

"Deliver this to Sabine."

He nods, taking the paper and nearly running from the room.

I reach out, fumbling. "Oh, no. That's okay. I can bring it myself. I didn't mean ..." But he's already gone.

The guard smiles at me, and it feels a bit patronizing, though I can't say why. "You are the King's Mate. You don't have to run errands."

Ugh. This guy.

With a huff, I turn to leave the library. I'll come back on my own sometime.

I wander the halls once again, looking for something familiar that can lead me to the stairs to the training room. I'd like to work off some of the tension that's coiling tighter in my gut. The impending Challenge hangs over my head and weighs down my steps, as if each passing moment settles another heavy coil of rope around my shoulders.

After an hour, I internally admit I'm hopelessly lost. I don't want to ask my guard, afraid he'll take it as an invitation to draw close to me, or worse, touch me again. So I keep walking.

Everyone I pass bows to me before going about their busi-ness, and I don't bother interrupting their day to ask for directions. I'm used to a certain degree of deference as the Lady of the Mountain clan, but this is on a whole other level. My neck is getting sore from the little bobs of my head in answer to all the bowing.

Maybe I should go flying. That would be nice. I saw a large lake at the eastern edge of the valley the other day, and maybe a swim through the freezing water will distract me. My body goes from tense at thoughts of the Challenge, to flushed at thoughts of Kem and me dancing in the clouds. But if things don't go well during the Challenge ... and I'm back to tense again.

The first door I find leading outside, I aim for it, my guard hot on my heels. I barely hold back my eye-roll. He'll probably shift and follow me into the skies. Doing my best to relax my shoulders down my back, I remind myself he's just doing his job.

The crisp winter air smacks me in the face, and I take a deep breath. The scents are muted in this form, but I'm learning the subtleties my human can pick up. A hint of lilac carries on the breeze, and under that, there's a dampness that suggests snow is on the way.

I practically skip down the stone steps until I'm rushing across a gravel path that looks like it leads to open meadows beyond the castle grounds. I kick off my boots in anticipation of the swim, flinging them under a stone bench.

My guard calls out, "My Lady, you shouldn't wander too far. The Challenge is in a few hours."

My jaw aches as I grit my teeth. *I know!*

The magic of the shift tingles across my skin like salt water lapping at heated skin. One breath in, my chest expands, and as I release it, my dragon unfurls. My wings snap out. My gold and amethyst scales glimmer and shine in the sunlight. I stretch, flapping my wings, watching the grass flutter.

"My Lady! You really shouldn't—"

With one great leap, I spear into the sky, climbing high. A low growl follows me, and a glance under my wing reveals the guard following me. His red scales flashing, his wings flapping furiously to keep up.

A smile pulls back my lips as I shoot through a cloud before angling along a current to carry me to the far end of the valley. I spread my wings and float across the sky. My body feels weightless as the push of the wind drags against the underside of my wings. Drifting side to side, I relax into the ease of simply riding the air.

Until my guard bumps my wing with his.

What's with this guy?

"My Lady, we should turn back."

I flap my wings, pulling away from him. "Not yet."

My stomach settles slightly as he nods, falling back, and when the lake comes into view, excitement pushes my speed. Drawing closer, I tuck my wings, scenting the water. Using my dragon sight to find a deep pocket in the lake, I dive, not caring if the guard follows or not. My head breaks the surface, and the freezing water slides over my scales as I stroke my legs to take me deeper. There's no following splash, and as I near the bottom, lake grass tickling my limbs, I roll over, catching the shadow of the guard flying overhead.

I smile again, bubbles dancing from my mouth toward the surface. A flick of my tail propels me along the lake bed. Soot and plants curl around my back. I shiver as a pocket of cold air presses against my scales, and I flip over in a lazy turn. A bubbling vent tickles my face where a natural spring feeds into this lake. I curl around the bubbles, following their path to the surface in a slow spiral.

The sun hits my belly as I roll onto my back, wings spread, floating with gentle swishes of my tail. The guard watches me from the shoreline, his posture ridged as he sits on his haunches.

I swim and float for another half-hour before diving deep once again. Calling on my magic, my skin tightens as my dragon shrinks. My bare feet punch into the lakebed, and I shoot upwards. My lungs burn, and my vision is hazy without my second lid, but my arms pull me upward with powerful strokes, and my legs kick with strength.

Sucking in a deep breath as I break the surface, the guard smiles as I swim toward him. His dragon wavers, shrinks, then the man stands at the water's edge, waiting. "Feel better?"

I can't help but answer his smile, because yes, I do. I nod, getting my feet under me, my clothes sticking to my body as I stride from the water.

"You can use your dragon fire to heat your body and dry your clothes."

Hmmm. I hadn't thought of that.

I focus on my center, feeling my fire stir. My skin warms and steam rises from my body. My clothes begin to dry as I comb my hair away from my face.

"Um, my Lady?"

I glance at him, and he nods at my shirt. I look down. Smoke is curling from the hem.

"Shit. Too much."

Pulling back on my fire, I just barely keep my clothes from catching fire.

My guard chuckles, keeping pace at my side. "Shall we walk back?"

I look down the valley, just now realizing how far the lake sits from the castle. I can't even see the gleaming spires from here. But I shrug. "Maybe for a little while. I need to waste the time."

The guard places his hand on my arm, his red nails like

blood against my pale skin. "I understand." His hand lingers, and I'm about to pull away from his touch, but his hand slides away—too slowly. There's a scrape against my skin, and when I glance down, the guard's nail, no, his talon punctures my skin, drawing blood in a thin line down my bicep.

My head snaps up. There's a little frown on his lips, and I think he's about to apologize, but he shakes his head with a shrug. I step back, stumbling, barely able to stay on my feet as the world around me spins.

"What ...?"

He reaches for me, but I throw up an arm. The movement feels sluggish, but I slap him away, stumbling back again. But this time, when the world tilts, I fall with it. I brace to hit the ground, but the guard's arms wrap around me, hauling me against his chest.

"Let ... me ghooo. Don't tousssh me."

A sharp tsking noise clicks near my ear. "We all have our roles to play today."

I struggle against his hold, but my limbs are too heavy, and the edges of my vision are closing in like Kem's shadows are wrapping around me.

I wish they were.

"Kemremeerer will ..."

"The King will be very busy all day. Plenty of people saw us fly away from the castle, me shouting after you in protest."

I shake my head, but it lolls to the side, draping over his arm. I blink several times as the grass swirls in dizzying patterns. My dragon roars in my mind, but the magic can't rise, like it's buried in heavy mud. I try again, begging my dragon to help, but she curls up, her head too heavy to lift, and as she closes her eyes, mine close as well.

I'm pulled down into the darkness that presses against my chest and paralyzes my limbs. I'm not sure how I'm even breathing around the oppressive gloom. In a last ditch effort, I search for the flutter in the center of my body where the Mate bond pulses.

I tug on it, but the flutter stays the same. There's no answering pull.

There's no help coming.

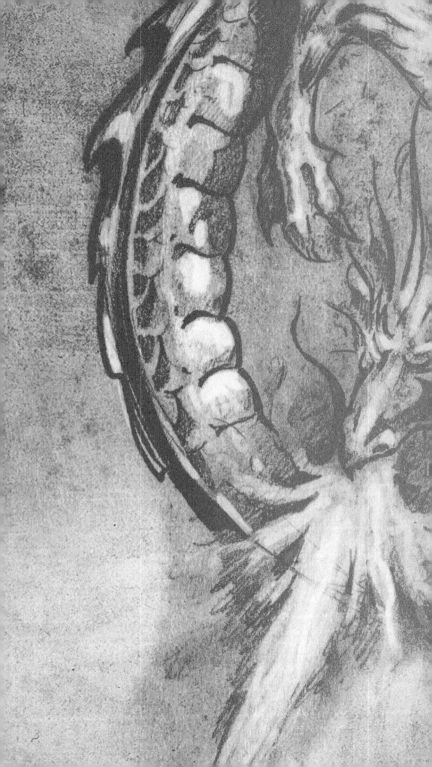

13

TATHA

I AM …

What? There's something I'm supposed to be doing.

I try to move my arms, but they don't respond to my brain's command. And wherever I am, it's dark. Wait, maybe my eyes are closed. I try to open them, but it feels like my eyelids are pasted together. I manage to wiggle a toe. A toe. So I'm in my human form.

My human form!

Internally, I jolt, but my body remains locked down. The lake. The guard.

The Challenge!

I grit my teeth, begging my arms to move. Nothing. *Please. Please.* I beg my dragon to break free, but she's still curled up, unmoving.

Fuck!

How much time has passed? I need to move!

I almost cry when my thumb twitches. It feels as if I'm buried in thick sludge at the bottom of the lake, but I continue to struggle, to fight.

I freeze as a muffled noise breaks the silence. It might be someone talking, but it's like I have cotton in my ears. Forcing my struggles to calm, I strain to listen. Slowly, the noise clarifies, and I make out a few words.

"How much ..."

"... just as you ..."

"... long will the effects ..."

"I'm not sure. This drug is untested." Rage swirls through my body, my dragon fire stirring. I know that voice. Inchel. "At least she's still out. If she begins to wake, dose her again with the same amount. We need her contained so I can take care of the King."

Okay. So, there's still time.

"And what will you do with her ... after?" At the sound of the red guard's voice, I instinctively try to clench my hands, but I'm still locked within the effects of whatever drug this is. That bastard!

Inchel clicks his tongue. "She'll be a bit ... broken after the Mate bond snaps." There's something like possession in his voice, and I fight against the bile that threatens to climb my throat and choke me.

An unfamiliar voice cuts in. "You're going to force a bond with her?"

Footfalls draw closer, and Inchel's voice sounds right next to me. "If it takes, she will be my consort and my way into the Mountain clan." A hand strokes down my arm, and I scream in my head. "I'm going to bring the clan back into the fold. They have too much freedom in their fortress."

The guard's voice wavers. "But they've always kept to themselves. Why—?"

A smack rings around the room we're in, and the guard stumbles back from Inchel's strike. By the echoes, I can tell this room is not very large.

Inchel's voice lowers with anger. "I'm not paying you to ask questions. I'm paying you to do a job. Give me the room."

It's silent for a moment, but neither man argues, and their footsteps carry them from the room, the door clicking shut behind them.

No. No. Don't leave me alone in here with him!

A shuffling noise brings Inchel's scent closer. His whispered words drill through my ears. "I'm going to kill Kemremir. You would be wise to submit to me once I'm King … for the sake of your clan."

Does he suspect I'm awake?

His lips press to my cheek, and his hand rests on my stomach, his fingers stroking lightly over the fabric of my shirt. The urge to sink my claws into his eyes trembles through my body to the point I'm surprised he doesn't feel it. But the drug holds me immobile.

He whispers again, "Hopefully, some of this is getting through." His lips brush the edge of my ear. "*You* are the reason I Challenged your Mate. I've been waiting years for my chance. I smelled his desire for you that day in the solarium. It's been a long time since the King lusted after anything. I know I can't win against him by strength alone, so I've waited. I've watched. All I needed was to find something or someone he loved"—his hand slides down my stomach and over my hip until his fingers grip my inner thigh—"and squeeze."

The screams in my head get louder as Inchel's fingers creep farther up between my thighs. "The King will do *anything* for you. Kemremir will die to save you. Once the bond is broken, I'm going to claim you, beautiful Tatha"—

Slimy wet heat slides up the shell of my ear as he licks me—
"whether you want it or not."

My throat burns with disgusted rage as his fingers brush
against pussy over my pants. His touch lingers before his hand
climbs, slipping the hem of my shirt out of the way. I want to
punch my claws through his chest and rip his heart out. His
lips trail down my neck and over my collarbone as his fingers
dip inside my pants. His breaths quicken, his nose nudging
the top of my shirt.

This is not happening. MOVE BODY. FUCKING MOVE!

A knock on the door brings a growl from Inchel's chest,
and I thank every god I can think of as the guard's muffled
voice calls from outside. "Counselor, the Challenge."

Inchel's fingers dig into my flesh just an inch shy of my clit
before he removes his hand, kissing the top of my breast.
"Later, my sweet Tatha."

Sharp clicking footsteps take Inchel from the room, and
the guard and second man file back in. A metallic slide and
click tells me this room is barred and locked from the outside.
How long will this drug last? I need to kill these men. I need to
get to Kem. I need to rip Inchel's head from his neck.

With Inchel gone, I can breathe a little easier, and I focus
on my muscles, trying to force feeling into my body.

The second man calls out from across the small room. "I
think her breathing is changing."

Shit.

Quick steps approach, and I feel someone leaning over
me, and the guard speaks right above my face. "Hmm. It's hard
to tell."

"Better dose her again, just to be sure."

"What if too much kills her?"

The second man laughs. "What if she wakes up?"

"The two of us should surely be able to subdue her."

"Don't be so sure. I've heard stories of this dragon."

The guard grabs my chin, turning my head. "Really? This little thing?"

"Just dose her."

No, no, no, no, no. Come on body! Move. Move. Move!

A sharp sting pricks my neck. My body gets heavier.

No, no, no.

"How long do you thi ... enge will ... st?"

"... ot long if th ... wants to save ... te."

Their voices die off as the sucking mud sensation pulls me deeper.

THE WEIGHT PRESSING in on me lessens slightly. I have no idea how much time has passed, and it takes me several precious moments to force some of the fog from my brain. I sink my claws into the darkness. Flexing every muscle, I pull. And I pull. And I pull. I have to get out from under this drug. I have to get to Kem ... if I'm not already too late.

With great control, I keep my body still as I drag myself out of the muck. I listen closely as sounds clarify. The air smells the same. I don't think they've moved me. A slight shuffling comes from across the room—the second man. The small smack of licking lips indicates the guard is standing behind me, maybe leaning against the wall.

Hmm. It seems this human form can pick up quite a lot if I concentrate.

But I need my dragon.

Working my way up my body, I test my movement. I concentrate on my toes and realize I'm still barefoot. I'm pretty sure I could wiggle them, but I stay still. A light pressure around my legs and torso tells me I'm still in my stretchy pants and top. The pads of my fingers brush against metal. I push down slightly, feeling the solid table under me.

A shuffling forces me to relax as the second man shifts his position, but remains where he is on the other side of the room.

I almost jerk as the guard speaks. "How long has it been?"
Good question.

A chuckle rings out. "Don't be so impatient."

"I just want this to be done."

"It will take as long as it takes."

The room goes quiet again, with only the little shifting and shuffling sounds of my captors. I catalogue my body, taking note of every tingling sensation as my muscles wake up. My feet and calves burn as the numbness wears off. Keeping my body relaxed and my breathing steady, I fight against the need to scratch my arms as they regain feeling.

I want to move. I want to shake off this awful pinprick sensation that's spreading over my body. But I stay still. I wait. I gather my strength.

My dragon opens her eyes, and my fire burns bright. Her head is too heavy to lift, but she's enraged. She wants blood.

And I will have it.

I will save my Mate.

14

KEMREMIR

I SWISH my tail against the dirt of the large natural amphitheater, looking for Tatha's amethyst scales.

Kudrer kept me in the council chambers for over two hours until finally, Syphe interrupted us, pulling me away. There was a small fire in the kitchen. No one was hurt, but one of the pantries was completely lost, and some equipment was destroyed. Not a huge deal, but with Moneria fast approaching, it's poor timing. So, I arranged for two of our cooks to travel to other worlds to gather whatever they'd need for the new year celebration. I also called in extra hands from the valley to help with cleanup.

Just as I was leaving the kitchens, Hiti jogged down the hall, her pinched face telling me another issue needed my attention. I nearly growled in frustration. Why was the kingdom falling apart, today of all days?

Hiti reported the main water line had burst. So, I spent the next hour organizing containment and repairs, and after, I had just enough time to clean up before leaving the castle, shifting, and flying to the northern edge of the valley.

My gaze scans the foothills that melt into the red grasses, framing the circle of hard-packed dirt where I stand. Dragons dot the climbing rocks and pepper the landscape with their brilliant colors.

But Tatha's brilliant purple scales are still absent.

Inchel's lime-green scales flash in the setting sun as he circles overhead once before landing with a great thud. The ground shakes, and his roar bounces off the rocks. Several dragons roar in answer, but I just smirk at him.

Such fanfare for a dead man.

Sitting on my haunches, I curl my tail around my legs, unconcerned with the dragon before me. He growls, and I laugh a puff of smoke at him. His lips pull back in a snarl, but the Eris, the master of ceremonies, steps between us, his deep magenta scales almost black in the fading light. Lifting on his back legs, Eris' wings flap twice as his voice rings out, "Silence!" A hush falls over the amphitheater. "Clan leader Inchel has issued the Challenge." I glance around again. No sign of Tatha. "This is a fight to the death. The winner will take the throne. This is Lord Inchel's first Challenge. This is Lord Kemermir's thirty ..."

I tune out Eris, looking more closely among the boulders and the crowd of dragons spread around us. She's not here.

I snap my head to Inchel, and his grin has my fire surging up my throat. "What have you—"

"The Challenge has begun!" Eris' proclamation drowns out my words, and he ducks as Inchel leaps into the sky, his wings flapping hard.

I don't think so.

Launching upwards, my giant wings carry me to my

enemy. The dragons roar behind me, the rules of Challenge keeping them grounded. My shadows spear out, grabbing Inchel's tail, but he flicks free. I need to get closer.

Inchel shoots into a thick cloud, and I smirk. His bright-green scales will be easy to pick out even in the cover of the thick vapor. I slip into the mists of the cloud, pulling my shadows around me. Drifting silently, I wait.

A disturbance in the air currents is all the warning I have, but it's enough. I tuck my wings, spinning, catching Inchel in my claws. I rake my talons down his side and dig my hind claws into his leg. He roars as we fall. The misty tendrils of the cloud whip by as the force of our descent pulls at my scales. I snap my jaws at his neck, but he twists away, getting enough leverage to slam his hind foot into my stomach, his claws sinking deep. A grunt of pain pushes from my chest, and I thrash my tail against his wings. Muscle and membrane tear under my assault, but he sinks his talons deeper, yanking up, tearing open my belly. I unfurl my wings, and with a groan, I pull us up and deeper into the cloud cover. The roars below get louder, the crowd upset at missing the fight.

I snarl into Inchel's face. "What have you done to Tatha?"

Magma drips from the corners of my mouth, and Inchel's scales sizzle and spit. He snaps his teeth at me, but I hold him back as more of my flesh tears under his claws.

"If you want your precious Mate to live, you will fall to me."

My muscles burn as I fight to keep us both in the air, but I push past the pain, rage fueling my body as I pull him closer, wrapping my tail around his throat. "I will kill you for touching her."

Inchel yanks his claws to the side, opening me up to my ribs. He pushes me, and the punch of pain spasms through my muscles, allowing him to rip free of my grip. He flaps backwards, just out of reach, but his breath is ragged, and his ruined wings struggle to keep him level with me. My shadows race across the space between us, ready to rip his wings from his back, but his scream stops me. "Kill me, and she dies!"

"Where is she?" My shadows pause, swirling with my rage, but holding back for now.

"It doesn't matter."

"WHERE IS SHE!"

He glances in the castle's direction, and I turn.

"If you disengage from the Challenge, you forfeit."

But she will be alive.

"I have people in place. If you forfeit to try to save her, she dies. If you kill me, she dies."

My mind races as we circle each other. Is he lying? If not, can I kill Inchel and get to Tatha in time?

Inchel smiles, and I roar. My fire erupts from my mouth, and the scales along his right side sizzle. He hisses in pain, the fire eating away at his right wing, but glee shimmers in his wide eyes, madness pulling a laugh from his throat. "You must fall. For the sake of your Mate." He backs away as I try to get closer, his wings beating double, his eyes shining with triumph. "I have you, Kemremir. The great shadow dragon will fall to me. To ME!"

I reach for the bond, searching for the flutter in my chest. It's there, but it's weak, sluggish. I get the feeling she's fighting; she's trying. Tatha is a fighter. She's my Heilsi.

I have to give her time.

One great stroke of my wings propels me forward. I tuck them into my sides, spearing past Inchel, who turns to keep me in his view. My tail slashes down his left leg as I pass, tearing through muscle.

The air currents carry the clouds away, and the sky darkens to the deep purple of the approaching night as Inchel screams after me. I slow, and just as I feel him swipe for my tail, I lift my chest, spreading my wings. The drag tears at the membranes of my wings, and a tendon snaps. Ignoring the pain, I think of Tatha as Inchel shoots under me before he can stop himself. Fire bursts from my throat, searing down his spine as I fall behind him.

I may not be able to kill him ... yet ... but I can cause him a substantial amount of pain.

I spit fire at his flank, but he spins out of the way, rolling onto his back and shooting fire back at me. My shadows intercept most of the flames, but a few burns my scales, and my stomach wound screams in protest. Blood shines on my dark scales from my abdomen down my left leg. Bright red drops trail behind me, and I know the blood loss is going to catch up to me soon.

Inchel charges, but I dive. The valley comes back into view, and the dragons bark and snap their wings, enjoying the show. Skimming the theater, I search for those amethyst scales.

Nothing.

I allow Inchel to catch up. Feigning right, I shoot to the left, dragging my tail across his snout. Blood sprays across his face, and he shakes his head.

Still no Tatha.

I find Syphe in the crowd. Her copper scales almost blend in with the rocks in the early evening dusk. Aiming for her, I'm distracted, and Inchel spears into me from the left. Grabbing my ankle, he drags me back, but I keep my eyes on Syphe. She tilts her head, trying to discern what my eyes are begging her to understand.

Inchel's wings give out, and he pulls me down with him. Still, I don't break eye contact with Syphe. Inchel turns so I'm under him when the ground slams into me. My left wing snaps, and his hind talons drive into my thighs as his front claws slam into my chest.

Syphe's eyes go round, and she breaks eye contact to look around.

Yes, please. Find her.

Inchel leans over. "I will make sure she's taken care of."

I throw my head back and roar. *She's mine!*

My claws sink into his chest, and my talons scrape against the bone of his ribs. He screams in pain, snapping his teeth at me. He glances to my right, and I follow his gaze. A rust-brown dragon nods almost imperceptibly at Inchel before making eye contact with a coral-scaled dragon. She nods at Inchel who then grins back at me. "She will die if you kill me, Kemremir."

I mean to pull back, but instead I sink my claws deeper into his chest. My dragon is pushing my human mind aside. All it wants is its Mate. My claws search for Inchel's heart, and I fight against myself.

She needs me to buy her time.

But my dragon shoves me aside. Shadows rip from my body, shooting down Inchel's nostrils, sealing his airway. I pull him closer, slamming my other claw into his neck, tearing scales, shredding muscle.

Movement catches my eye, and I catch the rust-brown dragon moving away through the crowd, turning toward the castle. Inchel leans into me. "Will you die for her? I can still stop Errot. Tatha can live."

I can no longer see Errot's rusty scales, and the coral dragon grins at me from the sidelines.

My dragon cries out for his Mate. The gentle flutter of our bond is weaker. My claws tighten, scrapping against bone, and tearing muscle, but my head falls back. Inchel snaps his jaws around my throat as one of my talons pierces his heart. We both freeze, and the theater goes silent.

Has Syphe gone to find Tatha? Will she be okay?

The driving instinct to shred Inchel's heart trembles through my muscles. I need to kill him.

I can't. I can't take the chance.

Inchel's muffled voice laughs from his hold on my throat. "Release me, Kemermir. Your reign is over, but she will live."

My dragon lets go. This is how we save her.

I call up Tatha's image, her beautiful face smiling in my mind as Inchel's jaw tightens.

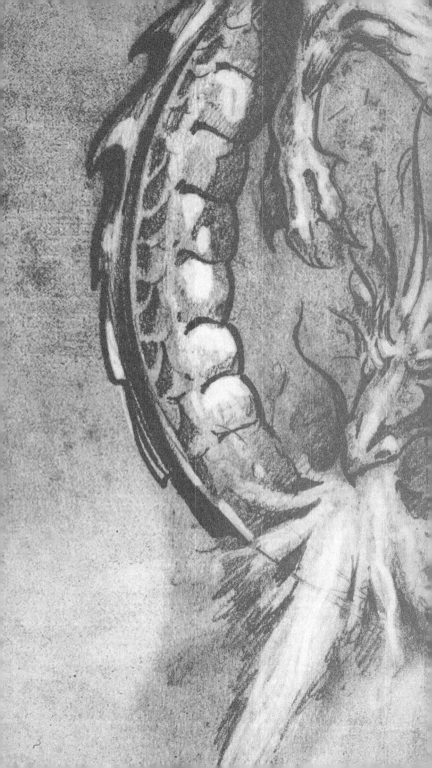

15

TATHA

MY DRAGON STIRS, her power thrashing through me the angrier we get.

A single knock on the door is followed by the click of the lock and the slide of the bar. The door squeaks as it opens, and a voice whispers, but I can't catch the words. Once the door is secured again, the second man calls out to the guard, "The Challenge has begun. It won't be long now."

I'm out of time.

The guard sighs. "Thank the gods."

"Relax, you'll get paid, and the new King will make sure you are most ... comfortable once he takes the throne."

Hoping their attention is on each other, I slide my eyes open to small slits. The room is just as small as I thought. Maybe twenty paces square. I can't shift in here without breaking several bones. What good will I be to Kem if my body breaks against these walls?

An idea curls at the edge of my mind, and I internally wince. This is going to suck.

Taking a slow breath, I call up an image of Kem. His dark eyes smile at me, giving me courage. I let a little moan slide from my lips, and I feel the men's attention land on me. The second man takes a step forward. "She's pulling out of it again."

"So quickly?"

"Dose her."

"That's a lot, I don't think—"

"Just do it!"

Yes, come here, little man.

I keep my eyes closed, letting my head fall to the side as I moan again. The guard's footfalls stop at the edge of the table, and I flutter my eyes open, pretending I'm struggling against the drug.

The guard shakes his head, leaning down. "Back under you go."

My dragon grins, her power flooding my veins. I grab the guard's shoulders, shifting my blunt human teeth into fangs. Biting down hard, I rip the flesh from his throat. Hot blood splatters across my face and pours down my throat. He jerks back, stumbling, and I follow, driving him to the ground.

I land on top of him, the room spinning slightly as the drug tries to hold me in a fog. The second male, large with deep teal hair, swears, rushing across the room. Before he takes two steps, I grab the guard's head and snap his neck. His body slumps under me, and I have just enough time to duck under the teal man's arm as he tries to grab me. I scramble to the side, and he follows. "Behave, little girl. Or your clan will pay the price."

I snarl, a low growl rumbling from my chest. "I don't think so."

Pushing off the wall, I barrel into his chest, wrapping my arms around his waist. He does the same, thinking to overpower me.

Stupid male.

I lean into his hold, snapping my leg up, kicking him in the face. His grip relaxes enough that I can roll from his hold. I crash into the door, yanking on the handle. It doesn't budge.

Hands grab me, claws digging into my skin as I'm yanked back. His arm wraps around my throat, cutting off my cry of pain and frustration. He squeezes, snarling, "You bitch. You're not worth the trouble. Inchel will get over it. There's plenty of whores out there."

His grip tightens, and his other hand presses to the side of my head, locking me in his hold. Little black specks dance in my vision reminding me of Kem's shadows.

My dragon roars. *Save our Mate!*

Panicked, I yell at her, *NO! Not here!*

My dragon shoves me aside and breaks free. There's a startled yelp of pain, and the splintering and cracking of wood echoes in the room.

Pure agony steals my breath.

My dragon immediately melts away, hiding from the blinding pain. I collapse to the floor, taking shallow breaths as I roll onto my side. There's a smear of flesh and blood on the side wall, and the teal man's crushed body lies unmoving on the floor. The guard's body is a pulpy mess as well.

Good.

I can't stop the scream from tearing from my throat as I push to my hands and knees, but I smile around my bruised and swollen face. The door is in pieces.

I attempt to crawl forward, but pain drives me back to the floor. My right arm is badly bruised, and my left shoulder is dislocated. My face feels like I flew straight into a mountain. I must have slammed into a wall or the ceiling when I shifted.

I take a shaky breath, and the dark dots in my vision turn white. My ribs are all either bruised or cracked. Surprisingly, my left leg is fine, but my right foot is turned at an odd angle. I grit my teeth against the sharp ache along the right side of my back. My right wing must be damaged.

Kem. I have to get to Kem.

Putting most of my weight on my left side, I maneuver myself enough to get my knees under me. I breathe through the waves of agony. Sheer desperation gets me to a seated position, and I poke my right ankle. It flares with white hot pain, and I hiss, "Fuck!"

I have to get out of this fucking room.

My dislocated shoulder protests as I grip the wall with my right hand, pulling myself up onto my left leg. The room begins to go dark, and sweat pours down my face, but I press my hand harder into the wall, forcing my body to remain conscious. I use the wall to hobble toward the shattered door, and once I reach it, I poke my head out, finding a dark hallway.

Okay, just get out. Get out. Get to Kem.

The hall seems never ending, but I drag myself along the wall. At the end, I rest the side of my face against the cool stone. Before me, there's a staircase leading up, and to the right of the stairs is a thick wood door.

Stairs or door? Stairs or door?

The thought of trying to get up the stairs has me reaching for the door. I prepare myself for it to be locked, but it swings open on silent hinges. Another narrow dark hallway greets me on the other side, this one longer than the last. But I smell ... lilac.

My stumbling hobbles pick up speed. The musty air

clears, and a slight breeze flutters against my face. My throat burns, and tears fall down my cheeks as a speck of light flares at the end of the hall.

Drawing closer, another door looms before me. This one has a barred window, and the soft light of dusk filters through. My palm slams into the door, and I grab the knob. It doesn't move.

"No!" My hand smacks into the door again. "Argh! Damn it!" The iron of the bars is cold against my skin as I grab them, yanking and pushing.

Nothing.

I can't shift here. This hallway is too small. It would completely shatter me. I throw back my head, screaming to the stone ceiling.

"Tatha?"

My head snaps down. Bronze hair flashes in front of the window. "Syphe?"

"Oh, thank the gods, I found you."

"Kem?"

Three metallic clicks vibrate through the door, then it swings open, and I fall into Syphe's arms.

"Shit, Tatha, what happened?"

I shake my head, shuffling to pull her away from the castle walls. "My shoulder. Can you pop it back?"

"Tatha, you need medical care."

I beg her with my eyes, and she nods, pressing her lips together. Gripping my shoulder and bicep, her fingers prod my joint, and I hiss. I would be flat on the ground if she wasn't holding me up.

"Big breath in."

I inhale, the pain of my ribs drowning out the pain in my arm. But then a scream rips from my lips as Syphe lifts my arm and shoves my shoulder back into place. The pain fades to a pounding ache, and I hobble forward.

Syphe tucks herself under my right arm, trying to steer me back toward the castle. "You need a healer."

"No!"

"Tatha, you can't walk on that foot. You're obviously in a lot of pa—"

"Inchel is using me against Kem. If I don't get to the Challenge now, the King might die."

Her eyes go wide, but I'm already reaching for my magic. My human scream morphs into my dragon's roar. I curl up on my left side, panting through the pain as my dragon assesses the damage.

Yup, everything hurts, but I'm a bit more steady on three legs, my hind leg curled up into my belly to keep my weight off my broken foot. I stretch my wings, and the right one twinges as muscles and tendons protest the movement.

Syphe's snout presses to mine, and I realize she has shifted. She presses herself under me, helping me stand. I stare at her, tears swimming in my eyes. Since I've come to this valley, I've cried more than I have in my entire life. Syphe doesn't know me that well. Yet here she is, helping me stand, helping me do what I need to do.

She asks, "Can you fly?"

I take a few shallow breaths, flapping my wings. Gritting my teeth, I nod. "I have to."

Launching into the air, Syphe follows, then spears in front of me. Her draft of air helps pull me along, and I'm thankful for the extra assistance.

A sprawled form on the ground catches my attention. I realize it's a man. His rusty hair spreads around his head as if he's sleeping, but there's a dark stain spreading around him, and his eyes are open and empty.

Syphe catches the direction of my stare and falls back, nodding at the body. "I intercepted Errot on my way to find you. He tried to kill me, so ..."

We fly past Errot's body, leaving him behind without another thought. I call out to Syphe. "Where is the Challenge?"

She jerks her head to the northwest. "There's a natural amphitheater in the foothills at the edge of the valley."

We fly straight toward the arena, and a sharp pull tugs at my center.

The bond.

Pain and sorrow that are not mine scrape along our connection, and it's like I'm being pulled to Kemremir by a physical tether.

I push through the pain and fly faster.

We skim the tops of the trees, aiming for the foothills. Frantic, I scan the skies, but there's no movement. Where is he?

Specks of color flash against the landscape, and the theater comes into view. There, in the center, Inchel leans over Kem.

The tether of our bond frays as Inchel closes his jaws around Kem's throat.

Syphe cries out in despair, but my roar drowns her out.

"KEMREMIR!"

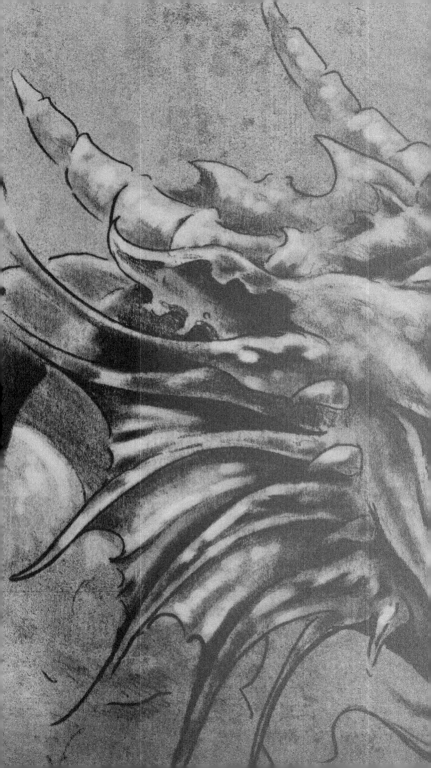

16

KEMREMIR

Tatha's outraged and pain-filled roar echoes against the mountains and spears into my heart. My Mate.

I can't see her. Where is she? Why is there so much pain in the bond? I need to see her.

Inchel's eyes go wide, and I roll us, shoving my claws into the flesh of his belly, my other hand reaching for his heart. Inchel tries to clamp down harder on my throat, but magma rumbles from my gut, spilling from the punctures in my neck before dripping from my mouth. The smell of burning bone wafts down my nose, and Inchel rears back, screaming in pain as my claws rip a hole in his chest. His fangs turn black, and a few of his teeth turn to ash as he whips his head back and forth, trying to get the molten fire out of his mouth. The tears in my throat burn, as they cauterize, but at least the bleeding has stopped.

"Kem!"

My head snaps toward Tatha's voice. Her brilliant purple scales are an intense midnight blue in the evening light. But the strokes of her wings are shallow, and her right wing bends at an odd angle. She hitches, her face drawn up in pain as she drops, and Syphe is there to catch her, keeping her from slamming into the ground.

A whoosh of air warns me, and I spin, ignoring every screaming stab of pain. I grab Inchel's tail; the barb sinking into the flesh of my right claw. Yanking, I pull him to me.

"No!" His scream of terror hangs in the silence, as every dragon seemingly holds their breath ... waiting.

My teeth close around the back of his neck. My shadows hold him still, his muscles trembling under my grip.

Tatha has shifted, and Syphe stands at her side, propping her up. My Mate's eyes bore into mine, her bruised face pulled back with determination. She hobbles forward a single pace, and rage floods my body as I take in her injuries, but she holds my gaze, standing tall.

She nods.

My teeth crunch into scales, flesh, sinew, and bone. Inchel roars, then with one hard jerk of my head, his roar cuts off. His neck snaps, and his limp body hangs heavy from my jaws. It's not enough. I grind my teeth, shaking my head until his spine severs in two. I chomp down once, twice, and Inchel's head flops to the ground. His long tongue hangs from his open mouth, and his quickly paling eyes stare into the void. I spit out his blood and chunks of bone with a wet splat onto the ground.

A chorus of roars lift into the night sky. "Long live the King! Long live Kemremir!"

I lift an eyebrow at Eris, needing this to be over—NOW. He steps forward, raising a hand. "The Challenge is completed. King Kemremir is the victor."

The roars grow louder in celebration, and I catch the flash of amethyst hair from the corner of my eye. I'm not done here. Not until Tatha is safe.

Turning a quick circle, I scan the crowd until I find the coral scales I'm looking for. She is skirting the outer edge of the theater, and her wings unfurl, ready to take flight.

Oh no you don't.

My shadows rip from my body, wrapping around her wings, crushing and pulling at the delicate appendages. She struggles in my hold, her head thrashing side-to-side, trying to see me coming. The dragons part, clearing a path as I stalk toward her.

Her panicked voice trembles. "I didn't have a choice! Inchel—"

My shadows dive down her snout, cutting off her words. Her eyes bulge from her head as she tries to take a breath and fails.

Walking up to her, I lean forward. "I don't care."

Her claws tear at her neck, trying to dislodge the shadows. I release her airway so I can hear her screams. And they are fantastically blood-curdling as I rip her wings from her back. I toss them aside, several nearby dragons scrambling out of the way as the pink wings smack to the ground.

Her screams grow louder, her eyes bulging from her face as my shadows turn her to face me. Faster than she can track, my arm snaps out, talons ripping across her chest. Her head falls back, her mouth open in a silent scream. I strike again, this time my claws sinking into her throat. Muscle and bone squish and crunch as I rip her spine out. I fling the bloody mess onto the ground, and the second my shadows pull back into my scales, the coral dragon's body crumples in a heap.

I make my way back to the center of the theater, unable to hide my limp as the pain of the fight comes flaring to life with the fading adrenaline. My eyes scan the colorful dragons until I find her. Syphe struggles to keep her hold on my mate until Tatha pulls free of my guard's arms, her limping hops bring her closer, her bare feet stumbling over pebbles and rocks. She ignores the carnage of Inchel's corpse, focused on me. I crouch, lowering to my belly, ready to shift, but before I can call up the magic, Tatha falls into my side.

I freeze.

Her small hands press against my scales. She's so small. I've been afraid of hurting her in her dragon form, but like this, I could crush her so easily. I'm barely breathing as she makes her way up my side. Her tiny feet squelch in the blood pooling from my stomach wound. My tail snakes out, giving her more of me to hold on to. Her fingers grip my scales, making her way up the curve of my neck. I shiver as her touch skims over my face.

When she comes around my snout, she presses both hands to my muzzle, and the purr that rumbles from my chest vibrates against the rocky round, pebbles skipping and jumping with the sound.

Her right toes skim the ground, and her ankle is dark and swollen. With every breath, a small wince pulls at her bruised face. But her eyes are fierce as she strokes my nose, staring at me. Her voice whispers across my scales. "Mate."

I feel that one word throughout my entire being.

She rests her forehead between my nostrils, and I breathe her in. Her hands continue to stroke me, and I can't help the stiffening of my cock.

A gentle voice cuts into our moment. "Sire, allow me to heal you." One of the royal healers, in his human form, approaches. I start to shake my head, but don't want to dislodge Tatha from where she's pressed to me. "In a moment." My shadows slowly peel from my scales, their power sluggish from my blood loss. "Tatha, let me."

Her head lifts at my grumble, but my shadows wrap around her, keeping her pressed against me. Her eyes pinch in confusion, but a moment later, she sighs. I have a small amount of healing power, but I usually use it through physical touch. Fear of hurting her further holds me absolutely still as I attempt to send my healing power through my shadows. The inky tendrils skim over her body, and I feel the pull and press of my power flowing through my shadows, easing her pain, knitting her torn muscles and tendons, and aligning broken bones.

Over and over, my swirling shades trail over her skin, reaching under her clothes to touch every part of her. Her pained breaths even out, then turn desperate. The scent of her arousal punches down my nose.

In this form, her scent is so much more potent. My fire burns through my veins, and my claws sink into the rocky ground. Fates, I want her. I force my voice to remain even and calm. "Better?"

She takes a deep breath, and a smile curls up her lips. "Yes, Mate. Much. Thank you." Her hands continue to pet my scales as she leans to the side, her eyes skimming down my long body. "You need a bit of healing yourself."

I huff, and smoke curls from my nostrils, drawing her attention back to my face. "Healer, go ahead." The man steps forward, shifting to his dragon. I keep my eyes on my Mate as the healer runs his clawed hands over my scales and wings. Tatha moves with me as I shift to the side so the healer can mend the giant tear in my stomach.

Tatha gasps, staring in horror at the wound, and when tears fall down her pale cheeks, I huff a breath of smoke at her. Her eyes meet mine, the sorrow in them nearly as painful as my actual injuries. To distract her, I ask, "The ones who held you?"

"Dead."

"Good girl." She shivers at my words, and a small smile lifts my lips.

The healer shifts back to his human form, bowing as he steps away.

I gently nuzzle Tatha. "Were there others?"

She nods, her vibrant hair spilling around her face. "There was someone delivering messages, but I never saw them. I'm not even sure if it was the same person or a different person each time. I was also drugged and passed out for a while."

I growl. "Did anyone touch you? Did Inchel ...? Were you ...?"

Her hand strokes my snout, quieting a fraction of my rage. "No. I mean, not that I know of. Inchel tried, but was interrupted."

My fire goes white hot, the blaze shining through my eyes, reflecting against Tatha's pale skin. "I'm going to hunt down the forbidden magic and bring him back to life to kill him again, slower this time. I'm going to track down every member of his family and make them pay for the sins of their brethren. I'm going to wipe every existence of Inchel from the face of our realm." Her eyes dance with fire as I purr, "We will find them—everyone involved—and we will kill them."

Lips parting, she nods. "Yes, Mate." Her chest rises with her panting breaths. Vengeance looks good on her.

"Now, shift."

Her eyes go wide, and she looks around the clearing. I don't have to look to know everyone has left, having tracked each dragon's departure.

It's just my Mate and me.

My growl deepens, the Mate bond snapping with my command, "Shift."

Her magic shivers over her skin, and I'm left breathless as her dragon unfurls. Her snout presses to mine, and we take a second to breathe each other in.

But then, my dragon rumbles, *Claim her.*

I back away, nodding to the sky. "Go, Mate. See how high you can get before I catch you."

Her tongue flicks out, and I playfully snap at her. A purr vibrates up her belly, and a curl of smoke escapes from her nostrils. Distracted by her dragon's beauty, I miss the slight bunching of her muscles, and in a flash, she's airborne. My tails flicks in excitement as I watch her climb the sky. The starlight reflects off her deep purple scales, the occasional wink of gold spectacular against the velvet night.

With a leap, I follow. My magic spreads like warm mineral water bubbling over my scales, finishing the last of the healing as I chase my Mate. The clouds have all blown away and scattered, so she weaves side-to-side, trying to evade me, climbing higher. Pulling my shadows around me, I hide in the darkness.

I swallow my chuckle as she glances over her shoulder, searching. "No fair!"

Her eyes dart around, and I glide under her. She scans the skies, frustration and annoyance pulling at our bond, but there's no fear. In fact, she's practically vibrating in anticipation. She wants me. She wants my dragon. She's not afraid.

My Heilsi.

The air is so thin this high, my brain feels fuzzy, or maybe that's just from being so close to my Mate. With one powerful stroke of my wings, I spear up behind her, my hind legs snapping out, my talons digging into the backs of her thighs. She gasps, but her tail wraps around my body, curling around mine.

Fuck.

The anticipation of taking her shivers through my entire body. I lean over her. "Are you ready to fall with me, Tatha?"

In answer, her tail tugs mine, bringing me flush to her ass. My pre-cum slicks along her entrance as I take us higher, her wings struggling to flap with me so close. I barely get any air with my next inhale, signaling we are too high—I don't care. My tongue slides up her neck, and she shudders against me. I can still smell Inchel's blood on our scales, and my dragon roars with rage and lust and triumph. Victory is mine, and I will claim my prize.

With a growl, I sink my teeth into the back of her neck, my cock jumping as her blood slides along my tongue. My front legs wrap under her wings, my claws sinking into her side and her chest. She roars, trying to thrash against the pain, but I hold her tight, sinking my fangs deeper into the flesh of her neck. Her claws sink into my forearms, the delicious sharp bite of pain melding with the pleasure as I keep us in the air, hovering at the edge of our atmosphere.

Ripping my teeth from her, a barking scream tears from her throat. I lick the punctures, purring against her scales, "Mine. Mate."

"Yours."

With one great thrust, I'm inside her wet heat. I feel her inner walls resisting my size, and she jerks in my hold as my cock stretches her. Seated completely in my Mate, my wings snap out, our bond thrumming with pleasure. She leans into me in complete surrender, pressing the tops of her wings to mine.

We fall.

She pulses around me as I slam into her, my pace picking up speed as we scream towards the earth. The pull of gravity pushes against my wings, and we begin to spin. I hold my Mate tight in my talons as I claim her among the stars.

Her moans are like a melody the night sky sings to me. I'm dizzy with wanting her, and our cartwheeling descent steals my breath.

Every thrust punches desperate words from her lips. "Mate. Yes. Kem. Fuck. Me. Mate. Claim. Me. I'm. Yours. Yours. Yours."

My grunts turn to growls, until the pleasure builds, and I throw my head back, roaring to the stars. Her pulsing inner walls grip me tighter, and I lower my head to watch her come apart. The world swirls around us, a blur of muted color and streaking starlight. But all I see is her. My Heilsi.

Blood trails up our bodies from our claws sunk deep in each other's flesh. She is dazzling, painted blood-red, gold, and purple in the night. "Come for me, Mate. Let me feel you soak my cock. Let the entire kingdom hear you."

My shadows curl around us, reaching for her clit, rubbing it hard. Her head snaps back into my chest, but I shove her forward with my snout so I can sink my teeth back into her neck in a claiming bite. Her mouth falls open on a silent scream that builds to a roar as her orgasm sweeps through her.

Pulse after pulse of her climax grips my cock, and as the ground grows closer, I shatter, my very being splintering apart in the euphoria of free-falling while coming inside my Mate. Sheer bliss shoots across every nerve as my cock slams inside Tatha's wet heat with jerking thrusts. Our mingled roars carry across the valley as the last of my orgasm fades.

The whistling wind gets louder, and when I dislodge my teeth from her neck and angle my wings to slow our spinning descent, I see the rocky ground quickly rushing up. For a moment, I think death might be worth it to remain deep inside in Tatha, but I force my talons to let her go. Sliding from her wet heat, we both groan as we twist away from each other.

The muscles in my back flex, and my wings strain against the drag as I pull up. The tall grasses actually tickle my belly, and my hind claws scrape the earth. That was a bit too close.

Tatha chuckles above me, her lighter weight allowing her to draw up faster. She spears away, speeding down the valley. Taking chase, my mouth waters as her tail flicks and her wings flap. She zooms past the castle before finding a low current of air. She glides on silent wings, aiming for the eastern lake.

She's fast, but I'm faster.

I pass over her, a dark shadow, and as I fly over the water, I tuck my wings. My magic tickles over my scales as I somersault, shifting in mid-air. The cold water slides over me as I dive deep, and a crash of water sounds above me as Tatha's human form dives after me.

I spin, floating up to meet her eager hands. She pulls me to her, and I kick us to the surface. By the time we reach the water's edge, I've lost my boots to the silty lake bed, and Tatha's small hands are pulling at my shirt.

We're naked under the starlight in record time. Pulling her mouth to mine, I devour her lips, tasting her. I fall back, bringing her with me, but she pulls away. Every pale, wet inch of her is on display. She runs her hands down my chest, landing on the now-healed scar running from my right chest all the way down to my hip. Her voice is low, angry. "So close. I came so close to losing you."

Pressing one hand over hers, I cup her cheek with the other. "You saved me."

Her amethyst hair floats around her face as she leans over, kissing the scar. Then her head lifts, and a wicked smile lights up her face. A deep groan slides up my throat as she spins, straddling my chest. I grip her hips, and she squeals as I pull her ass over my face and yank her soaked pussy onto my eager mouth. My tongue spears into her, licking up every morsel of her arousal, and her back arches, pressing her breasts into the night air.

She falls forward, her small hand wrapping around my cock, and I growl against her clit as her hot mouth slides over the head of my shaft. Her hips press into my face, grinding against my beard, and I growl again, letting the vibration rumble against her clit.

Her cheeks hollow out as she sucks me deep, and my fingers dig into her hips as I pull her tighter against my lips, my tongue shifting so I can delve the forked end even deeper into her delicious heat.

Glittering droplets of water steam off our bodies with our heat, and before long, sweat slicks between our sliding skin.

Her tongue swirls around the head of my cock, and she cups my balls as she strokes down my length with her other hand. I slide a finger between her cheeks, gathering her wetness and some of my saliva before circling her tight hole. She pops off me with a gasp, pressing back into my probing finger.

My purr rumbles all the way to my cock. "Oh, Mate. I can't wait to take your ass with my cock as my shadows fill your dripping cunt."

"Fuck!" She slams down on my face, and I laugh, licking her as I slide the tip of my finger into her ass.

Her lips curl over her teeth, and she drags her mouth down my length, sucking hard. My balls draw tight, and my finger slides further into her ass. I curl the tip of my finger as my lips close over her clit, and I suck her down. Lifting off my cock, she throws back her head, her hair swaying as she screams her orgasm to the stars.

I lick my lips, my words muffled against her sweet cunt. "So beautiful, Mate."

Her smile hits me as she looks over her shoulder. Throwing her leg over my chest, she kneels between my thighs, gripping my cock. I prop myself on an elbow, needing to see her swallow me down. Her lips hover over my aching head. Her eyes slide up my body until she looks at me through her long lashes. "Fuck my mouth, My King."

I shoot up, curling my legs under me until I'm kneeling before her. "Heilsi." I thread my fingers through her hair, gripping the soft strands close to her scalp. She moans, and I tug her head back. My voice is deep with emotion. "You own me. Completely. Body, heart, and soul. I'm yours."

She swallows, her throat bobbing with her head held back. "Yes."

Fisting my cock, I press the weeping head to her lips, pulling her head down the length as I grind my hips forward. I only go halfway before pulling back. Without warning, I pull her face toward me, slamming my cock to the back of her throat. She gags, spit dripping from the corner of her lips, but she wraps an arm around my hips, grabbing my ass to hold me deep in her mouth.

I purr at her. "My Mate wants more?"

She can't speak, but she attempts to swallow, her mouth sucking me deep. Gripping her tighter as her hot mouth contracts on my shaft, a growl slides from my lips. "Fuuuck me!"

I pound into her, transfixed at the sight of my cock sliding in and out of her swollen lips. Her other hand dips between my thighs, gripping my balls. My body convulses as her eyes lift to meet mine. Tears glitter on her lashes, and saliva drips down her chin.

My hand tightens in her hair, slamming my cock down her

throat over and over until I shatter with a roar. She swallows me down, but cum still leaks from her lips as I continue to jerk with my release. With one final thrust, I slide from her mouth, pulling her hair as I drop to the ground, bringing her to my chest. She moans as I massage her scalp, and I feel her open her mouth, stretching her jaw.

"Was that too much?"

She props her chin on my chest; her smile brilliant as she licks the last of my cum from her lips. "Not at all. It was just what I wanted."

I drag her up my body, kissing her, tasting my release on her lips. "You are everything I wanted and more." I caress her face, my fingers trailing along her delicate features. "I'm sorry you were hurt."

She nuzzles her cheek into my touch. "I handled them. You handled Inchel. I'm just sorry I was a weakness that almost cost you your life."

I bring my other hand to her face, framing her jaw. "Tatha, understand. You. Are not. A weakness. You didn't need rescuing. You are fierce. You came to me. You gave me the strength to win. You are my Heilsi."

She releases a breath, brushing her lips against my palm. "I love you, Kemremir."

I press her head onto my chest, combing my fingers through her hair, kissing the top of her head. "I love you too, Tatha."

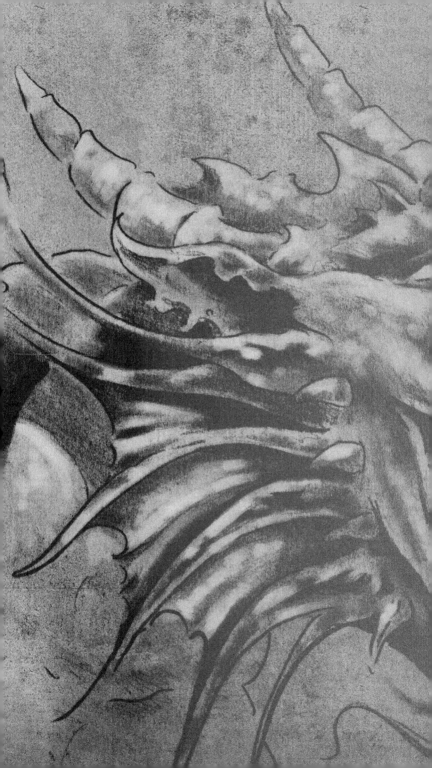

17

KEMREMIR

TWO WEEKS LATER

I TAKE a deep breath of crisp winter air. Snowflakes dance and twirl on their downward journey from the clouds. Tatha tilts her head back, blinking as the fat flakes caress her face before quickly melting. I wrap an arm around her waist, hugging her to my side. Leaning down, I kiss a few melted snow flakes from her cheek. Her fire, cinnamon, and earth scent wraps around me, and I grip her tighter, my purr bringing a chuckle from her lips.

When she angles her head toward my face, I lean back, unable to stop the small frown from pulling at my lips. "Are you sure, Tatha? There's no rush. We can—"

"Yes, I'm sure." Her fingers ball in the fabric of my shirt, pulling me down for a kiss. The moment our lips meet, I'm lost to her. She shifts back, her breath teasing over my lips. "Moneria is a celebration of new beginnings—you are my new beginning."

My hand slides into my pocket. "I was going to wait until later, but now seems right." My fingers gently grab the delicate petals of the small flower. Reaching out, I tuck the nesaea flower behind her ear, the tiny white petals almost lost in her vibrant curling hair. Tatha's fingers tremble as she lifts a hand to caress the petals. "How did you find one? It's not even close to their season."

"I had a few seedlings waiting for next summer. A little magic coaxed them to bloom early ... for you." She tugs at my shirt, and I lean down again, nipping at her lips. "Mate." My tongue curls over her bottom lip. "Heilsi." I press a gentle kiss to her mouth. "MINE."

"Always."

My arms wrap around her small body. Small but fierce. Our kiss deepens, and she melts into me.

"Kem!"

I smile against Tatha's lips before lifting my head. My Mate turns, but I keep her tucked into my side. Syphe releases Raelyn's hand as they pop through the dragon magic that allows us to travel between worlds.

Rae sprints toward me, her long dark wavy hair flying behind her. I can't help but chuckle as her crown cants to the side and starts to slide from her head in her haste. She doesn't break stride as she pulls the wayward crown from her head and tosses it at the silver-haired male behind her.

Her husband, Asheraht, drops his hand from Syphe's shoulder, fumbling to catch his wife's crown. The king of the

Seelie fae grins like a fool at Raelyn. She has that effect on everyone. She's a burning ball of light and energy and kindness.

Tatha looks up at me with a smile, and I loosen my grip enough to allow her to wiggle away. She is only a single step back before my arms are filled with a squealing fae. Raelyn's arms wrap around my neck, hugging me tight. I hug her back, and she giggles. "I'm so, so happy for you, Kem."

"It's good to see you, your Majesty."

Her head snaps back, and I hold her for a second longer before she drops to her feet. "Oh no, none of that!"

Ash comes up behind Rae, his roguish grin still in place as he bows to me. "You know better, Kem. Rae doesn't like when her friends actually acknowledge she's a Queen."

Rae playfully slaps Ash on the shoulder. Turning back to me, she tucks her dark hair behind her ear, glancing at Tatha. "So, introduce me."

Before I can answer, my Mate steps forward, bowing low. "I'm Tatha. Thank you for coming, your Majesty. It was very important to Kemremir that you were—"

Raelyn grabs Tatha's shoulders, hauling her into a hug. "I'm so honored to meet you."

Tatha's shoulders relax, and her arms return Rae's embrace. "You're just as Kem described you."

Ash laughs. "Kem has probably left out a few things." His hand brushes down Rae's arm, and she steps back into him, keeping a hold of Tatha's hand. "She can be a terror. Trust me."

I laugh, and Raelyn shoots us each a stern look, but her lips tremble where I know she's holding back a laugh of her own. Jabbing an elbow into Ash's stomach, Rae tugs Tatha down the stone steps toward the snow-covered gardens. "Tell me everything ... how you two met, all this business with Inchel ... what a fucking asshole."

Tatha laughs, lacing her fingers with Raelyn's as they disappear around a hedge of winter roses, their blooms closed tight against the freezing air.

I turn to Ash, and he holds out an arm which I take in a firm grasp. "Thank you for coming."

"Are you kidding? Nothing would have kept Rae from being here today." His fingers comb through his snow-damp-ened hair. "And well, ..."

"Where she goes, you go."

His cheeks flush as he shrugs. Raelyn and Ash went through a lot before they found their happily ever after. I'm glad I didn't kill him.

We release our clasped grips, and I turn, leading us down a long walkway to the castle's great hall. Ash stomps his boots and shakes his head, dislodging the snow before stepping through the open doors. I grab a mug of ale off one of the many tables lining the side wall. "Drink?"

Ash smiles, swiping a mug and taking a big swallow. "One of the main reasons I'm here, my friend. Dragon ale is above and beyond any I've had."

"Of course it is."

Ash laughs. "Of course. Still humble I see."

"Confident."

Ash takes another swig, the foam sticking to his dark stub-ble. "So, you nervous? Oh, wait. I forgot who I was talking to. Of course you're not."

I chuckle, shaking my head. "No. Not really. Just hoping I can be everything she needs."

The crinkles at the edges of Ash's eyes smooth out. "You are her match. You are the other piece to her soul. Just being there for her is enough."

A cloud of sadness passes over his eyes, but it's gone the next moment. Still, I grip his shoulder. "You and Raelyn may not be fated Mates, but you are each other's hearts. You know this."

Ash nods, taking another sip of ale. When he pulls the mug away from his lips, his smile is back in place. He turns a slow circle, whistling. "You've gone all out."

The floor-to-ceiling windows gleam in the cloud-covered sunlight. Evergreens drape over the doors, windows, chandeliers, and tables. The marble floor is bare except for a purple and black rug at the end of the room. The weave is intricate, with vines and swirls dipping in and out of our colors. Firelight sways from torches lining the room as well from the hearth at the opposite end of the long room.

And the flowers ...

Ash leans over, breathing in the delicate scent of the large orchids on the table next to us. "Beautiful."

Indeed. Flowers of every sort permeate the entire room, adorning tables, hanging from golden planters, and spilling from tall vases flanking the doorways.

"We have several solariums in the castle where we cultivate both native plants and plants from off world. Tatha and I met in the east solarium."

Ash smiles, looking around the room, taking in the multitude of colorful blooms. "Has she seen it yet?"

I shake my head, setting my mug down and clasping my hands behind my back, hoping to hide the sudden nervous flutter that jumps in my chest.

Ash nods. "She'll love it."

I smile, looking around. I hope so.

Ash and I talk, catching up as people start to file into the room. Everyone bows as they enter, then mill about, carrying on their own conversations. The room fills quickly, and yet more people arrive, spilling out the open doors onto the stone patio and down into the gardens.

My hands clasp tighter as I notice several members of the Mountain clan conversing outside in small groups. I know they won't come inside, but just the fact that they are here *and* in their human forms shows how much love Tatha's people have for her.

Leaning toward me, Ash draws my attention. "Has everything from the Challenge ... been sorted?"

Clenching my hands isn't working, so I stuff them in my pockets. "For the most part. We found three more who conspired with Inchel to"—my voice drops, rumbling with a growl—"use my Mate."

Ash has a few choice words for Inchel, and my mind drifts, recalling when we found the woman who ran messages to the men holding Tatha. My Mate didn't hesitate, shifting in a flash and stabbing her tail through the woman's heart. After, she flicked pieces of flesh and blood from her scales, and I arranged for the body to be burried. Traitors don't receive the honor of cremation. Their ashes will not float up to the stars. Their remains will rot, locked under the earth. A few days later, we found two others—one who set the kitchen fire, and the other who broke the water line. I quickly took care of them.

My gaze scans the room, landing on Kudrer. He bows when he catches my eye, then quickly steps outside. The indigo male has made himself scarce since the Challenge, but I can't find any concrete evidence that he was directly involved. And he's too smart to incriminate himself ... so far.

Ash pops a thin slice of roasted meat into his mouth, licking the fat from his lips. "Well, if you ever need help ferreting out conspirators, let me know. I'm very good at finding and extracting information."

I grin at the former assassin, though I doubt his elevation to King of the fae has stopped the man from keeping his deadly skills honed.

"I'll keep that in mind."

We drop the topic, choosing instead to speak of happier things—mainly our women.

I try to stay focused, but I can't keep my eyes from flicking over Ash's shoulder, watching the daylight slowly fade. He keeps talking, telling me tales that I'm sure are well embellished, but I recognize he's trying to distract me, and I'm grateful.

Then, the magic in the room swells, the firelight flickers before getting brighter. My guards step into the room, and the crowd parts as they march down the center, each wearing their black leather armor with my flame symbol over their right breast. Arvun, Undreth, Hiti, and two others flank the aisle leading to the empty rug at the end of the hall. Syphe comes in last, her copper hair pulled back into her customary intricate braid. She smiles at me with a nod as she joins her fellow guards.

Rae slips into the room, crossing to us, a huge smile lighting up her face. She kisses Ash, and he wraps an arm around her waist. Turning to me, her grin expands until she's practically glowing. Her hair dances around her, and the ale in Ash's cup floats into the air as her magic flares with her joy.

Ash presses a kiss to her cheek, and she blushes. "Sorry." The air settles, and the ale sloshes back into his cup. "I'm just so happy for you, Kem. She's wonderful."

I smile. "Thank you, Raelyn. She is wonderful."

Ash claps me on the back. "Show time."

The room goes silent as I stride across the room, between my guards. The click of my boots on the marble sounds overly loud in my ears until I cross onto the rug. My soles sink into the deep pile, and I take a deep breath, turning to face the far end of the room.

As King, it is my responsibility to perform the Mating ceremony for those lucky few who find their true match. I think of Syphe and Bran's ceremony. Their joy and love affected everyone in the room as my magic imbued into the cuffs they chose, allowing the bands to shift with them between forms.

The doors swing open, and I forget how to breathe. Tatha steps into the room, her hand resting in the crook of her brother's elbow. Her eyes find me, and I swallow the fire burning in my chest. She's wearing black. A tight-fitting bodice adorned with tiny black crystals hugs her waist and presses her breasts up. Layers of sheer black and grey fabric drape from her waist to trail the floor. The sheer fabric swirls around her legs, layered to make the skirt opaque, but the strips of fabric part as she walks, revealing tantalizing slivers of skin.

The dress looks like my shadows, and as that thought crosses my mind, the tendrils peel away from my body, swirling around me, reaching for her. Tatha's bright smile nearly buckles my knees. Why is it taking her so long to get here?

Kogra kisses her cheek, but her eyes remain on me. My shadows caress her first, then I take her hand as she steps next to me. "You look glorious, Mate."

My shadows dance around her dress and smooth along her amethyst hair, playing with the curls. She laughs, the sound filling the large room with warmth and happiness. "You're not so bad yourself."

My black pants and grey sleeveless tunic seem drab next to her. She runs her free hand down my chest, her fingers trailing the purple and gold embroidery. "It matches my colors."

I glance at Ash before smiling down at Tatha. "I'm your match."

A beautiful blush colors her cheeks and chest. I want to consume her. I want to claim her. I want to fuck her right here.

She leans in, whispering, "I know that look. Soon enough Mate." She looks around. "Thank you for the flowers. They're beautiful. It's like the first day we met."

"You put them all to shame, my love."

She smiles, ducking her head.

Turning, I hold Tatha's hand as we face the crowd. "I, King Kemremir, claim before the gods and my people that Tatha of the Mountain clan is my heart, my soul, my Mate."

In answer, a low vibration sounds around the room and spills in from outside—my people rumbling with the magic of their dragons.

Tatha's grip tightens on my hand. Her chin lifts, and her voice is strong and clear as she faces the crowd. "I, Tatha of the Mountain clan, claim before the gods and my people that King Kemremir is my partner, my heart's desire, the missing piece to my soul, my Mate."

We turn back to face each other, and her eyebrows scrunch together, whispering, "You said you'd handle the cuffs?"

I smile, holding our hands up between us. "I've got it."

My shadows swirl down my arm, curling up hers, and with a push of my power, two tendrils break free. One wraps around Tatha's left wrist, swirling in intricate patterns around her creamy skin. I turn her hand, exposing the underside of her wrist. Reaching into my pocket, I pull out Tovra's grey scale. Tatha gasps as I push my magic into the dead scale. Spring green colors the edges before spreading. The green darkens until the scale shimmers a vibrant shimmering emerald. I press her father's scale to her wrist, and my shadows curl around it, securing the small piece of her father into the Mating cuff I made her.

The other piece of shadow curls around my wrist, and Tatha lifts her head. Her eyes swim with unshed tears. "It's perfect."

"You're perfect."

A tear dances on the edge of her lashes, and I brush it away before leaning in, taking her lips in a deep kiss. The room erupts in cheers and roars, but all I can hear is my heart slamming against my chest and Tatha's breath against my lips.

Finally, we pull away from each other, facing the crowd once more. I raise my hand, the shadow cuff swirling around my wrist like it's showing off. It probably is. I sure am.

Everyone quiets down, and I clear my throat. "Please join us at the North Lake."

The people outside start to shift, dragons leaping into the sky. The rest of the crowd moves outside, shifting as well. Bran holds Ash in his claw, and Rae climbs on Syphe's back. Tatha and I shift at the same time, spearing into the air.

The dragons part as we touch down at the edge of the North Lake. On the eastern edge, set back from the water, we approach a large orchard. Trees of every size and shape spread before us—trees from our world, and many from the vast amount of worlds in our universe—each one planted on Moneria and nurtured by the dragon's magic.

I reach into the well of my magic, retrieving a small seed. Tatha steps closer, staring at the seed. "Is that ... a mountain pine?"

I nod. "Seemed fitting the mighty pine of your home should be planted the year I found you."

She rests her claw over the seed in my palm, brushing her cheek against mine before stepping back. I cross into the orchard, scooping a hole in the dark earth. Dropping the small seed, I gently cover it, patting the soil. Turning, I look over the crowd. My people sit back on their haunches, every eye on me. Ash and Rae stand next to Ziza and her wife, the couples wrapped in each other's arms, smiling at me.

I flap my wings, lifting onto my back legs, and every dragon does the same. Magic pours from our bodies, seeping into the ground, feeding the orchard, nourishing the new seedling.

I drop to all fours, and everyone settles as I clear my throat. "Moneria is upon us. With the new year, remember you have the power to take your life in a new direction if you so desire, for the future belongs to those who believe in their dreams. Tomorrow will be the first page of a new chapter—you decide how to fill those pages." I turn to Tatha. "Make them interesting and filled with love."

Dragons take to the skies, Ziza and Arvun scooping up Rae and Ash this time, as we all head back to the castle.

We shift back to our human forms, and the night passes in a swirl of drinking, dancing, and laughing. Tatha walks the gardens and the patio, greeting and thanking each member of her clan for coming to the valley. The snow and ice crystals cling to her skin and dress, making her look like a dark snow queen.

I take every opportunity to kiss my Mate, tasting the whiskey I made sure was in plentiful supply tonight since I learned she prefers the amber liquid over wine. I also make sure to feed her plenty of food. She's going to need the energy soon.

An hour later, I glance around the room from where I'm seated, Tatha nestled in my lap. Her voluminous skirts hide my erection, but I know she feels it as she shifts her ass every so often. I lean over her, kissing her behind her ear. "Where's Rae and Ash?"

She chuckles, rubbing against me again. "They slipped away a while ago. Rae said they have the time to stay a few days, so I arranged a room." She leans back into my chest, tilting her head back, giving me better access to the long column of her neck. Her throat flexes under my lips. I glance over, and her lips smile with a wicked intent, whispering, "I can only imagine what they're doing."

That's it.

I stand, my arm keeping her pressed against me. Leaning down, I growl in her ear, "Get them out of your head. All you should be thinking about right now is how I'm going to claim every orgasm I wring from your sweet pussy."

Her lashes flutter, and I inhale her arousal as I move us forward through the revelers. Many are too drunk to notice our passing, and I'm glad my people are enjoying the night. It's a celebration, after all. But some smile, bowing as we pass, knowing whispers trailing behind us.

As we cross through the doors, I lean down. "How do you want me, Mate?"

Tatha stumbles at my whispered words, gasping, but I hold her up with a smirk. She's had a bit too much to drink, and she's adorable as she scrambles to get her feet under her and moves forward, faster now. "So many ways, but right now, I want you in the solarium."

I can't hide my surprise, expecting her to take us to our bed. She loves sex in her human form, and our bed has been her haven these past weeks. But I'm all for pleasuring my Heilsi wherever and however she wants. I take her hand and run down the halls. She giggles after me, at one point kicking off her shoes to keep up.

The heady scent of the solarium reaches me first, then the

glass room comes into view. It's a little barren since most of the flowers were moved to the great hall, but it's still lush with greenery. As soon as we cross the threshold, my magic snaps out, sealing the door and the hallway, making sure no one disturbs us.

Tatha's skirts swirl around her legs as I spin her, slamming her against my chest. My hands trail down her bare shoulders and along her arms. "You are so beautiful, Tatha."

I lift her up my body, gripping her ass through the thin fabric of her dress. She grinds against me as our lips crash together. I lick her tongue before prodding her mouth, thrusting like I'd like to do with my cock.

But her scent is overwhelming.

"I need to feast on you, Mate."

She moans, fisting my locs. My shadows wrap around her, lifting her higher, and her moans turn into a gasp as I shove my face between her thighs. "Wrap your legs around me, Tatha."

Obediently, her legs drape over my shoulders, her thighs squeezing my head. My shadows hold her up, and I keep a firm grip on her ass as my shadows peel the strips of her skirt to the side, baring her to me.

I groan, nipping at her flesh. "No underwear. All night I was this close to heaven?"

My shadows slide between her folds, holding her open to me. My tongue laps at her sweet center, and she bucks into my mouth as my shadows curl deep inside her. "Yes, Kem! I've been so wet for you all night. Please. Please."

I lick her again, flicking my forked tongue around her swollen nub. "Easy, Heilsi. I've got you."

I eat her like a man starving. My knees go weak at her taste, and I leave red marks on her ass from gripping her so tightly. I glance up. Her body heaves with pleasure. Her chest thrusts against her dress, and her head falls back, her amethyst hair swaying against the dark fabric of her dress. Sharp screams burst from her mouth with every pass of my tongue, and I'm bewitched. I need to watch her come.

My teeth graze her clit, and she jolts against my hold, pressing her cunt into my greedy mouth. I suck ... hard, swallowing her gush of release, licking her through her first orgasm of the night.

The first of many.

My shadows ease her down, continuing their strokes and pulses inside her. She pants as I hold her against my chest. "I need you, Heilsi."

Her eyes sparkle as she tilts her head back. "Then bend me over that chair and take me, Mate."

Fuck, this woman is perfection.

"As my queen demands."

With her hands braced on the arm of the chair, her ass in the air, the skirts of her dress sway around her hips as she comes around my fingers, on my tongue again, and then finally around my cock. I take her against the glass wall and let her ride me on the cool marble floor.

Eventually, we make it back to our rooms, where I feed her fruit and chocolate, licking her lips clean before I crawl over her naked body. She arches into me, and I take her nipple into my mouth. Her moan of pleasure is the sound I'd like to die to. I hold her gaze, my fingers stroking her face as I slide into her wet, sensitive pussy.

"I love you, Tatha."

She takes me, all of me, staring into my eyes. "I love you, Kemremir."

We come together and fall into a sweaty heap, legs tangled, chests panting for breath.

After a few moments, she rolls off the bed, padding toward

the bathroom, but pauses. Her eyes go round as she notices the scrolls on the long table against the far wall. Her head swivels, looking over her shoulder at me. "What's that?"

I grin. "The first of your order."

She looks back at the table. "Three? Already?"

"Sabine is the best in the Realm."

"Hmm."

I'm not sure how to interpret that noise.

She hurries into the bathroom, returning quickly to settle in the bed curled against my side. My fingers comb through her hair, and she sighs. I've learned this is one of her favorite things, and I love how her body melts against me when I stroke her hair and massage her scalp.

"I feel bad. I don't think I'll have much use for those scrolls." She nuzzles against me. "This human form is growing on me. And ... and I like it here."

My heart swells with joy—more than I've ever experienced even on my best flight. "That makes me very happy, Heilsi. It's up to you, but maybe we can bring the scrolls to your Mountain. You can house them there; start building up the Mountain clan library."

She sighs, and her cheeks press against my chest with her smile. "I like that. I like that a lot." My fingers continue to comb down her hair, and her breaths slow down, tickling the hair on my chest. Her sleepy voice curls around my heart, my very soul. "Mate."

"Go to sleep, my love."

I hold her, staring at the ceiling. Never did I dream I'd be so fortunate, but here I am ... Mated. Happy.

Tomorrow, I'm surprising Tatha with a trip to her Mountain. I'm bringing Rae and Ash too. I can't wait to celebrate our Mating all over again in the great caves of her home.

But for now, I hold my Mate in our bed.

I kiss the top of her head, and she snuggles deeper into my chest. Curling around her, I let myself follow her into sleep. The last thing I see before my eyes drift closed is our shadow cuffs, swirling around our wrists.

Perfect.

Did you skip book one to get straight to the spicy dragon
goodness? I don't blame you, not at all.
But if you're curious about Raelyn and Asheraht and their role
in Kem's past, I encourage you to go back and read book one,
The Elemental

ALSO BY T. B. WIESE

Scan the code below for links to my Amazon author page where you'll find the first book in this series as well as my other books.

You'll also find a link to my website for signed books and swag.

ACKNOWLEDGMENTS

A big thank you to my readers who begged and pleaded for more Kemremir. His story was in the back of my mind, but your love for him pushed me to put his story to the page. So, thank you! We all needed more of the shadowy Dragon King.

To all my beta readers, thank you! You had a big hand in making this novella what it is today.

And lastly, I want to thank all my friends and family for cheering me on and being as excited about my characters as I am—I love my tribe.

ABOUT THE AUTHOR

T. B. Wiese is a military spouse, dog mom, photographer, Disney nerd, and lover of spicy fantasy. She loves animals (She grew up with dogs and working with horses, including working at the Tri-Circle D Ranch at Disney World), so don't be surprised when you find yourself reading lovable animal characters in her novels.

If you'd like to keep up to date with future releases as well as new swag and sales, sign up for her newsletter via link in code below.

SCAN THE CODE WITH YOUR CAMERA APP FOR HER SOCIAL LINKS